PLEDGE YOUR LOYALTY

THE ILLICIT BROTHERHOOD

PLEDGE YOUR LOYALTY

THE ILLICIT BROTHERHOOD

GAIL HARIS // ASHTON BROOKS

Pledge Your Loyalty
By Gail Haris and Ashton Brooks
Copyright © 2022 Gail Haris and Ashton Brooks

Note: This story may not be suitable for persons under the age of 18.

Cover: Lou Stock
Photographer: Michelle Lancaster
Model: Benjamin Adkins
Formatting: Elaine York- Allusion Publishing
www.allusionpublishing.com
Editing and Proofreading: Rebecca- Fairest of All Book Reviews and Elaine York- Allusion Publishing, www.allusionpublishing.com
Proofreading: Rumi Khan

Trigger Warning
Pledge Your Loyalty is a dark, college romance that contains explicit sexual content, graphic language, and some situations that readers may find uncomfortable, such as murder, blood, death, self-harm, violence, snakes, and alligators. We hope you enjoy this secret society of possessive alphas and the girls keeping them in check.

ACKNOWLEDGEMENTS

Thank you so much!!! We hope you enjoy the first installment of The Illicit Brotherhood, and are eager for more. There's still so much more we have planned...

We owe a huge thank you to Kiki and our readers for pushing us to write together. This has been such an amazing and fun project. Thank you to Rachael, Jill, Colleen, and the supportive team at The Next Step PR. A very big thank you to our hype teams and beta readers. You all have been incredible, and we couldn't have done this without any of you.

Thank you to the team at Give Me Books. Vilma Iris. All the bloggers, bookstagrammers, and people who have shared and supported this adventure.

A huge thank you to Lou J Stock for our amazing cover and crest! You helped bring this world to life. Michelle Lancaster for working with us on capturing our vision. Ben is the perfect Steffan. You're all so talented and we're in love with this cover!

Thank you to the most amazing women with the best set of eyes! Elaine, Becky, and Rumi. You're all three the best!! Thank you for helping us get this story to where it is and helping it become the best version.

Our Shameless Sisters (Shucky Darn Crew), friends, and famil: thank you for constantly supporting us. We owe you all everything! Lots of love!

xoxo

Gail & Ashton

THE ILLICIT BROTHERHOOD
GLOSSARY

The Illicit Brotherhood: A secret society of elite powerful members. Members are intertwined through high social positions and the underground world of crime. All are wealthy and extremely dangerous. There is a president and every family picks a 'head' to represent them at meetings.

Founding Families: The original founding families are: Suco, Concord, Carmichael, Boudreaux, Van Doren, and Dupree.

Original Bloodline: This refers to descendants of a founding family. Killing a member from an original family is a harsh offense. It must be voted on between head family members. If a family does something to disgrace or go against The Illicit, one remaining heir may live and strive for repentance.

Delta Pi Theta: A social fraternity at Thorn University, in Blue Rose, Alabama. This fraternity is the training base for the future of The Illicit Brotherhood. Founding families send their male heirs to rush this fraternity. The brotherhood also grows through new members and molds them to fit The Illicit. They form bonds within the brotherhood and establish their roles.

Scabs: Pledges of Delta Pi Theta

The Blue Tie: Delta Pi Theta brothers wear royal blue ties to all meetings and social functions. If a brother becomes serious about having a partner and bringing them into the know of The Illicit Brotherhood, they give them their blue tie. This lets everyone know not to pursue the person as they are 'claimed.'

PROLOGUE

Halloween
Thorn University, Sophomore Year

Steffan

You know what you need to do.
   For the brotherhood.
   My father's words repeat in my head as I stand on the outside balcony of our fraternity home. "For the brotherhood," I scoff to myself. My entire life has been *for the brotherhood*. Sometimes I think the sole purpose for my existence is to carry on my father's legacy as the leader of The Illicit Brotherhood. Since my twin, Soren, is clearly not planning on getting his shit together anytime soon, my father has marked me as his heir...the one to take over his precious role as leader of the secret society built upon blood, greed, and control, by any means necessary.
   This is my second year at Thorn University in Blue Rose, Alabama. It may not seem like a location for grooming future crime lords, but here we are. Delta Pi Theta. We appear to be a social fraternity in a small town in the South. In reality, we're so much more. The future of an elite secret underground society.

The founding families have sent their heirs here since the sixties. One doesn't have to be from the original bloodline to rush for Delta Pi Theta, but it helps. I'm the first member ever to go from a pledge straight to fraternity president. I am the son of Rhett Carmichael, after all. He gained his power in ranks by brute strength and force. After the founding family decided to step back, my father wasted no time in seizing the reins. And now that he's claimed it, he fully plans to maintain control, *at any cost.*

Scanning the crowd for my frat brothers, my eyes seek the glowing masks we coordinated for our fraternity's annual Halloween party. Delta Pi Theta never does anything less than the fucking best, and tonight is no exception. People may not know exactly what we are, but they know *who* we are. The best of the best. The elite. This fraternity is the golden ticket to a life of wealth and privilege. *But at what cost?* We don't share that detail. However, those who survive the four years in the brotherhood at Thorn University have already proven they'll do anything, and give anything, to be, and remain, at the top.

Despite the slight fog rolling off the nearby swamp grounds, I find my brothers easily, at the corner perimeter of the party, watching, always staying alert. For trouble. For a possible threat. For a potential client...or target. To everyone around us, Delta Pi Theta members appear to be just a group of friends partying. No one sees who we really are...the predators among the prey. That's the way we like it and want to keep it.

As members of The Illicit Brotherhood, the double life we lead on our college campus requires us to blend in, to act like normal college kids, while also helping our families run an underground empire. One that requires loyalty from one another and our associates. Unfortunately, tonight, I am going to have to remind one of our own what happens when that loyalty is broken.

I slip my mask back over my face and head inside the old but elegant mansion that is our frat house. It's secluded from the rest of campus, and unlike some of the Greek houses, ours is completely owned and funded by the founding families of The Illicit Brotherhood. This house holds weapons, secrets, and probably more money than the entire town of Blue Rose. But nobody outside of our organization is aware of any of that. Even within, only the fraternity brothers of Delta Pi Theta, who have proven themselves, are privy to all the information that this fortress holds.

The sea of partying bodies separates as I make my way down the stairs and through the house to the backyard. The smell of beer and bonfire hits me the second I step onto the grass. I stride quickly through the circled-up crowd of students, hovering near a makeshift DJ stand and the bed of a pickup truck, doubling as a bar, in order to reach my brothers.

As if sensing my presence, or maybe it's just that twin thing, Soren finds me first. Our identical eyes collide, and I silently communicate the burning anger under my skin that I'm attempting to keep locked down. He tilts his head in my direction before Lee Concord, one of my closest friends, Delta Pi Theta brother and future business associate, turns toward me. I give them both a slight nod as they slide their masks back over their faces, the blue paint covering the skull mask emanating enough of a glow that it's easier to move through the darkness.

"Where's Bryce?" Soren asks under his breath, his legs moving in sync with mine, as we move farther away from the crowd.

"I saw him down here earlier," I murmur back, my eyes focused forward, my mind completely consumed with the task at hand.

"So, it was true, then?"

I glance sideways at my twin, his eyes barely visible under the mask, but I can feel the anger radiating off his body. I glance again at Soren and pick up my pace. I don't have to speak; Soren knows me better than anyone, and without another word, he follows in line behind me.

"Fuck," I hear Lee say under his breath. None of us wants to believe that the Van Doren family would cross us. Now Bryce, another member of The Illicit Brotherhood, needs to be made an example of. His father's indiscretion is a death sentence and grounds for complete exile from the organization for the rest of his family. Bryce will be punished, stripped of all the benefits and status that comes with being a part of our organization. The Van Dorens are done, and it is up to me to make this known to the rest of the brothers. A nice little reminder to members that you don't fuck with The Illicit. This will also fuel rumors about our organization and restore fear, letting word spread throughout the campus like wildfire that you don't cross Delta Pi Theta.

I spot Bryce right away, his mask sitting on top of his head while he chugs a cup of keg beer, grinning and laughing with some of his football buddies. Anger sizzles in my veins the closer we get to him. I'm wound tight and on edge, while he appears carefree and way too relaxed. He's probably buzzed, but I'm about to sober him up real quick. I'd bet money that he has no idea his father was just busted and taken out by mine, or that his family is about to lose everything for crossing The Illicit Brotherhood.

One of the football guys notices us first, a look of panic crossing his features before he turns to Bryce, making him aware we're heading his way. I catch a look of surprise in Bryce's eyes, probably because I never actively seek him out. We may be fraternity brothers and associates of The Illicit Brotherhood, but we usually stick to our own friend groups. He excuses himself from his teammates and the busty brunette who was under his arm, before walking toward us. I can smell the strong odor of liquor on him and see the glossiness of his eyes now that he's standing in front of me.

"'Sup, brothers?" He greets us, raising his hand up for a high five, and I push down the urge to knock him out right now. None of us move to reciprocate the gesture. His face burns red, the smirk on his lips faltering, until he drops his hand completely. The three of us circle him, and then surround him, forming a cage. We step into his personal space and stand against him, completely emotionless underneath our glowing masks.

"Something wrong, guys?" Bryce asks, fear lacing his words.

"Are you fucking kidding me?" Lee pops off. I shoot my arm out to keep him in check when he goes to step forward.

The party has gone from robust with a loud mix of hip-hop and rock music to an eerie hush of whispers and the crackling bonfire. Not trusting myself to speak, I motion for Bryce to follow us. His mouth clamps shut, but he does as instructed. I wave my finger in the air to signal for one of the brothers to turn the music back on as I stalk off, putting as much distance between the party and us as I can, choosing to head toward the trees by the swamp, so we'll be hidden.

Once I spot the clearing, I turn to Lee. "Stay here." He stops, nodding his head in understanding. I need him to be our lookout, to make sure we weren't followed and that none of Bryce's teammates decide to check up on him anytime soon. Soren falls behind Bryce, making sure he doesn't try to make a run for it. Bryce's footsteps falter slightly, realizing he has nowhere to go, but he's smart enough to keep his mouth shut.

When I'm sure we're far enough out, and I can't see Lee, I stop and turn to face Bryce.

"Dude, Steffan, what's going on, man?" He laughs nervously, his eyes moving between Soren and me.

I scan him up and down, taking in his defensive posture, his legs spread apart as if preparing to run, his hands turning to fists at his sides. "Are you playing stupid, or did you really not know what your father was up to?"

Bryce shakes his head. "Look, brother, whatever is going on with my old man, I had no part of it."

My mind flashes to the images sent by my father. Some of our best workers have been tortured and killed after refusing to keep Jacob Van Doren's indiscretions secret from the rest of the families.

"But you knew."

"It's just a little skimming off the top. My father's company was having a hard time this last quarter. He planned to pay it all back," Bryce argues, and I can tell from the way his eyes widen a fraction that he believes the lie he's telling. *That, or he's a damn good manipulator.* The thought has me tilting my masked head slowly to study him. Is he trying to play me for a fool like his father did mine? Soren chuckles darkly. There's my answer. I glance at my masked twin, who is slowly nodding his head. *He's trying to play us.*

Tsk. Tsk. Van Doren or not. No one is safe from The Illicit Brotherhood. I give a single nod to Soren before turning back to Bryce, my arm swinging, and my fist connecting with his jaw. Bryce stumbles back from the impact, his face morphing into a mix of surprise and fury.

"What the fuck, Steffan!"

"If you think I believe anything you have to say, especially about your piece of shit father, then you must be stupid, Bryce," I tell him, fighting to keep my voice even. "As of right now, I'm here to let you know that you're out. The Van Dorens are no longer associated with The Illicit Brotherhood. You get one chance to leave tonight and never return."

"Or what?"

Soren pulls out a knife. The blade gleams in the moonlight. Slowly, he takes the point of the blade to his chin and then drags it down his neck, all the way to his torso. Showing Bryce exactly what could happen to him. I grab Bryce by the collar of his shirt and hiss through clenched teeth, "We will carve you like a fucking pumpkin."

"This is bullshit!" he yells back, staggering as I shove him away. "You think you can disown me? Our family has done more for The Illi—"

"You're a snake, Van Doren. And as for your family..." I pull out my phone and bring up the video my father sent earlier—proof that Bryce's family was not only stealing money from our organization, but going to extreme lengths to cover it up—and shove it in his face.

Bryce glances at my phone before looking back at me. "It's not what it looks like! Those people were lying..." he trails off when the video shows *his* father pushing a woman into the bed of a semi-trailer. Then he turns and opens fire on the men that he had been doing business with.

I feel my blood heat at his words. "This is a massacre." Turning the phone back to me, I press the screen and then flash him the image of the piled-up bodies again. "A cover-up. When I eliminate workers, it's when they're a danger to The Illicit. Your father was covering his own ass. It's weak and pathetic. You're done, Bryce. You and your family."

I shove Bryce back, my skin crawling from having to even be near him. "Pack your bags and leave. Your time here at Thorn University is done."

Bryce falters before catching his footing. When he glances up, he has a crazed look in his eyes and an evil grin on his face before he laughs, slightly manic sounding, and I feel the hairs on the back of my neck stand up. Time holds still for a minute, and in slow motion, I watch as a switchblade swings an inch in front of my face, as Bryce's body slams into me.

"Steff!" I hear Soren yell, but it's too late.

My instincts kick in when my back hits the grass. Bryce swings his arm, and I block each blow, careful to avoid the blade.

His face contorts in anger, becoming more and more red each time he misses. I'm able to push him up and land a punch to his jaw, and even with Soren yelling to Lee in the background, I never take my eyes off the metallic gleam of the blade. My hand reaches out, and I grab Bryce by the throat. His body momentarily freezing, and his eyes bulging. I could end him right here if I wanted to. It would be so easy to say things got out of hand and he left me no choice. Bryce definitely has no guilty conscience when it comes to trying to kill me. I can hear my father's voice in the back of my mind, though, reining me in. We only take a life if there is a purpose. Killing is messy, and to kill another member of The Illicit, even with Bryce's family's sins stacked against him, would still require an explanation and an investigation from the head of each family. Both of which I don't have time for, and neither does my father. Bryce's life is being spared out of respect for his grandparents, who were founding members, and he will be given a second chance to restore trust, even though I doubt he'll ever earn it back.

Reluctantly, I ease my grip and throw Bryce off me. "Killing me won't change anything. Your father already accepted his fate, just fall in line."

"If you think my family will just go away quietly, you're mistaken," Bryce yells, before lunging at me again. This time, I use my own momentum to send us rolling, while I use my knee to knock the knife from his hand. Bryce rears back, reaching for his ankle, and pulls out a gun.

My hand shoots out to grab it right as Soren comes running and then rams into Bryce, shoving him off of me. His body lands with a splash on the bank of the swamp.

"What the fuck?" I scramble to my feet, my hand grabbing Soren's arm. "He had a gun."

"I know!" Soren grits his teeth, turning to face me. "Why the hell didn't you just snap his neck?"

"You know the rules," I growl back. My hands rake through my hair, my mask long gone. We both stalk toward where Bryce is struggling to get up.

"Fuck the rules," Soren declares, before kicking the gun from Bryce's hand and landing a jab with his knee to Bryce's chest, pushing him farther into the swamp. Soren displays his disgust and spits into the water, his eyes ablaze with anger and hatred as he stares Bryce down.

Bryce manages to get up. His clothes soaked, his lip bloody. With clenched hands, he screams, "You'll pay for this!"

"You just tried to kill us!" Soren yells back and moves to follow Bryce into the swamp, but I grab his arm, halting him.

"He's not worth it," I remind him, knowing full well *what he's planning to do. It's too risky.* "Dad said..."

But Soren doesn't care what our father told us. The eyes behind the mask have gone dark as they narrow at me, and he jerks his arm free. He's backing Bryce farther into the swamp and splashing the water with his hand. My eyes flash to Bryce, whose mouth opens to yell more obscenities. I'm about to pull Soren away when Bryce lets out a scream that will be ingrained in my memory forever, as he quickly disappears under the black water with a splash.

"Allison thinks he's worth it." Soren jogs toward the edge of the swamp, and I follow. The water bubbles, and Bryce's head resurfaces. *Allison... No.*

"Help me!" Bryce roars out in pain.

Bryce goes back under, and I can hear the gnashing of teeth. "Shit!" I run back.

"The fucking gator has him," Lee yells.

I turn to Soren. "Where's the gun?"

Soren's hand comes up to his head, fingers grabbing his hair, while his eyes stay transfixed on the water that is churning and splashing. Bryce's cries are muffled between gargles of water and the slap of the alligator's tail, as it attempts to hold her prey under.

"Over there!" Soren finally yells to me, while I search frantically in the reeds and brush.

Fuck. Fuck. Fuck!

My heart races and adrenaline rushes through my veins. My eyes can't focus with the splashing dark water and the way my lungs are forcing me to gasp for each breath. My foot connects with the metal of the handle, and I reach down to pick up the gun. Without second-guessing it, I run into the murky water, causing enough commotion to hopefully distract the beast. I aim everywhere around where Bryce is frantically trying to swim away. I keep shooting until the chamber is empty, each shot causing water to spray up. Bryce cries out, his hand reaching toward me. I grab him and pull his body over to the edge of the bank.

"Help me, Sor!"

He finally moves and grabs Bryce's other arm. There's blood dripping from the corner of Bryce's mouth and a tinge of a metallic smell in the air.

"We should just leave him," Soren huffs at me. "The Van Dorens are a bunch of traitors."

"You know I can't!" I bite back. "The hell were you thinking pushing him into the swamp." *He knew there was a chance Allison would be there.* Shit. We have to get Bryce out of the water and stop the bleeding.

Soren scoffs. His eyes cut to Lee, then back to me. "I saved your ass. We pledge loyalty, remember?"

I'm freaking out. What will be the consequences if Bryce lives? What if he doesn't? Are there witnesses? Is my unhinged brother now in danger? I hear Soren's low voice next to my ear, "I was doing what you couldn't get done."

For a moment, I fear he's right, that my father would approve of his method, that he's stronger than I am. No, I'm following protocol of The Illicit. Going rogue causes more problems than necessary. I'm angry I'm questioning myself, because I must maintain control. *I am the president of Delta Pi Theta. I am the future of The Illicit Brotherhood.*

"Were those gun shots?" one of the fraternity brothers asks as he runs toward us, pulling his mask up. I watch his face turn pale when he shines the light from his phone and notices Bryce. "Guys..."

My gaze follows his, down Bryce's body to where his pant leg is torn, the flesh is ripped to shreds, and the bottom half of his leg is gone. "Shit!"

"Belt!" I yell to Lee, pointing to his waist. Lee's hands are quick as he pulls the leather through the loops and hands it to me. I rush to Bryce's leg and wrap the belt tightly above the wound. "Call 9-1-1! I need more fucking light! Now!"

Lee grabs his phone and starts dialing with shaky fingers. Soren uses his phone to provide light. Bryce's whole body is wet and muddy. His eyes open and close, his breathing turning labored as he begins quivering either from the pain, the cold, or the fact that he's going into shock.

"If the blood loss doesn't kill him, infection probably will. Might want to clean that wound," Soren snarls.

"Get off my back," I shush my brother. "Shit, Soren. I'm sorry. I'm trying to at least stop the bleeding. *Fuck.*"

"Stop panicking. It won't be the end of the world if this piece of shit dies."

"It was an alligator." I hear Lee explaining to someone on the phone. I remove my sweater and place it over Bryce's wounded flesh, adding pressure.

"An ambulance is on its way," Lee assures me.

"*Fuck.* What are we going to tell the cops?" I ask Soren.

"Not too late to toss his ass back in the swamp."

"Absolutely not. We have witnesses," I speak through gritted teeth.

"I'll call Dad," Soren tells me, and I shake my head. I'm not prepared to deal with my father. I fucked up. I was in charge and let things get out of hand. I lost control of the situation. In his eyes, it will be a complete failure. This whole situation is a giant clusterfuck.

"You need to get out of here," I tell him. "Now!"

Head members of the families will ask questions, they'll know about Allison and why we have her. They'll know that Soren knew it was dangerous pushing Bryce into the swamp. In fact, they'll think he did it on purpose, with the intention of killing him. *Did he?* We have a code within the brotherhood. We had orders to punish and banish Bryce Van Doren, but not to kill him. He is still part of a founding family, an original bloodline. Worse, my father will ask how and why I let the whole situation go to shit. My qualities and abilities to lead will be questioned. I can't have this blowing back at us.

"What?" Soren asks confused.

"If Bryce dies, they're going to be after you. Dad will have to find a way to clean it up. You need to leave," I tell him, my voice becoming urgent and rising in frustration. It's only a matter of time until more people from the party come this way once the EMTs get here. If Bryce lives, he'll try to pin this on my brother, and I can't have that either. It's better if Soren disappears before help arrives.

"Get out of here, Soren!"

My brother rears back, rejection flashing in eyes that are almost identical to my own. It kills me to hurt him, but I need to save him, which means, until we know what will happen with Bryce, Soren needs to go away. Taking my advice, he gets to his feet and stalks off, avoiding both me and Lee.

"How are we going to play this?" Lee asks, his eyes focused on Bryce, who is now passed out from the pain. I keep my fingers on his pulse at his wrist, and my other hand presses against his wound, trying to stop the bleeding.

"I don't know. Either he lives or he dies, then we decide from there."

"I'm in no matter what," Lee responds.

I nod my head at Lee's loyalty.

We protect our own against anything.

Dulce periculum.

CHAPTER ONE

Thorn University, Junior Year

Steffan

"I have eyes on him. Try not to worry about it. Just concentrate on the new pledges that are coming in this year," my father instructs, his voice sounding as authoritative over the phone as if he were in the same room with me and not a thousand miles away. Rhett Carmichael has that effect on people, and as his son, I'm not immune to his power. Fear of disappointing him is what caused me to spend a year in fucking misery and regret. No. I won't blame him. It was all on me. I was a coward, and I live with that self-hatred and regret every damn day.

"Father. I've explained this time and time again. I acted rash. Soren—"

"Is where he needs to be, just like you're where you need to fucking be. Do *not* argue again with me on this. You did the right thing."

No. If I had, I wouldn't be questioning that night every day since. I should've stood next to Soren in a united front. My father jumped at the opportunity to send him away. I've never understood their animosity with one another. Soren has always been viewed as the disturbed Carmichael, the bad twin, a freak, and some have even mistaken him as "slow."

He's quiet, yes. He uses action rather than words ninety percent of the time. And he is one of the most intelligent people I know. But he does have a wall put up. He only ever let himself get close to our mother, and...well...me. But that was before I sent him away.

"The pledges, son." My father reminds me in a tone that lets me know he isn't speaking to me anymore as my parent but as my boss.

I close my eyes and pinch the bridge of my nose, hoping to ease the pressure of the headache I can feel forming behind my eyes. I hate the beginning of a new school year for one reason alone...new pledges. It's just like my father to use that as a distraction, so I quit questioning him about Soren.

"Yeah," I tell him, keeping my voice as calm as possible, "should be an interesting crowd this year."

"Keep them in line," my father warns, and I feel heat creep up my neck at his underhanded comment. "Also, that present I bought you arrives next week."

"I'll look for it," I respond in code, knowing he is referring to the large shipment of guns and ammunition that will need to be picked up in seven days and handed over to some of our partners. Using a college campus for our operation provides the perfect, neutral setting for these types of deals to occur. The whole fraternity is made up of different members of influential families that are considered allies to The Illicit Brotherhood. For four years, it is a male heir's job to attend college here, pledge Delta Pi Theta, and serve the fraternity, which also means working for The Illicit Brotherhood. The brotherhood is slightly chauvinistic like that, only sending their sons to be the future members of their secret society. But using the front of a fraternity makes it easier to hide from the rest of the campus, who does not know we exist. Since our allies all have a child or relative here, the campus is heavily guarded. Any move against us while here would be a direct declaration of war to The Illicit Brotherhood. The five families from The Illicit also send their children to Thorn University, so that we have the chance to work together with our allies, building trust for future dealings. After Van Doren's fall from grace last year, my father has been even more cautious with the information he shares and who he trusts. Plus, you just never know who could be listening in on your phone calls these days.

"Good, son," he says. "I'll call next week."

He hangs up before I can respond, but I continue to stand with the phone pressed to my ear, the silence deafening.

"I take it he didn't give you anything on Soren?" Lee asks from where he's leaning against the pool table in the living room of Delta Pi Theta, our fraternity's house.

I shake my head, not trusting myself to speak. Everything's changed since last year. Where my father has grown more guarded and suspicious of his partners and allies, I've had to learn to let people in more, and by people, I mean Lee. It was up to us to set the tone for how the campus would run after the mess with Bryce, and his many allegations that led to an abundance of rumors. Bryce lived after the alligator attack. Unfortunately, he lost the lower part of his leg. Due to the injury, he was unable to play football any longer and lost his scholarship. He hasn't returned to campus, and if he's smart, he'll stay away. Next time, he might not get so lucky and live to tell his tales. Though his surviving saved us the trouble of owing The Illicit Brotherhood an explanation and requiring law enforcement involvement, it didn't stop mouths from gossiping. My father had to intervene because the rumors were so bad.

I was then tasked with making the decision about what would happen to Soren. It was the hardest day of my life. Not only had I made him leave campus but I also agreed it would be better if he left the country. I'll never forget the way Soren looked at me that night, like I betrayed him, but I needed him safe. He hasn't talked to me since. I haven't had the chance to tell him why I made him leave instead of backing him. He's my twin, my other half, and I will always do anything to protect him, even if it's from himself. And a part of me did freak from the crazed look in his eyes. *Would he have actually gone through with killing a fellow brother?* Van Doren is a dick and knew about his old man, but wouldn't we have done the same if it had been our father? Are we any less guilty for the shit we do? Sure, we can argue we have lines we refuse to cross. Our hands are far from clean. I could and would have killed Bryce if necessary... *Fuck.* Too much happened and I wasn't in the right headspace. Because of my second of panic and fear about straying from the protocol, my brother and best friend is now giving me the ultimate silent treatment from halfway around the world.

Ever since we were younger, there has been something off about my brother. I can't remember when I first noticed the ghosts in his eyes, but I do remember that emptiness and rage vibrating just beneath the surface from when we were kids. He ran off one day and didn't return until dark. My mom was worried, thinking he had been kidnapped by a rival organization or gang. My father found Soren and brought him home. Soon after, Soren quit talking. It took years for him to start speaking again. I was the first one he spoke to, and then my mother, until eventually short, clipped sentences to everyone. But he never told us why he ever went silent to begin with. He never voluntarily had normal conversation with anyone. Always to the point or an asshole remark is all we can ever get out of Soren. Whatever happened back then caused him to live recklessly. Soren is the first to take a dare, the first to jump into a fight, and would stand in front of a loaded gun if it meant taking a bullet for someone he deemed worthy. He also never sleeps, avoids going home unless it's demanded of him, and he rarely speaks to anyone. Except for me and Lee. So when he has something to say, we always listen.

But it's that recklessness that got us into the Bryce situation last Halloween.

And it's why he had to go.

"He has eyes on him," I finally answer Lee, shaking my head. "Whatever the hell that means."

"So, no idea if he's actually doing okay?" Lee's brow rises.

"Just that he's breathing."

"I heard you talk about the pledges." Lee twirls the pool cue in his hands. "You heard the new names last night, right?"

I smirk. "You mean that a Suco is pledging this year? Yeah, I heard. As you can probably conclude, I didn't share that with Father Dearest just yet."

Lee snorts. "With as paranoid as he and my dad have become, I wouldn't yet either."

The Illicit Brotherhood is an organization run by six powerful families: the Concords, the Sucos, the Carmichaels, the Boudreauxs, the Van Dorens, and the founder's family, the Duprees, who are still around but not as active anymore. They haven't had a son or daughter born into the family in almost forty years. Now that Bryce and his family are out, the rest of us are left to carry on until a new family can fill the spot, a ritual that our fathers would oversee. It just so happens that in the next few years, the Carmichael, Concord, Suco and Van Doren members will have sons who are attending college. When Soren, Lee and I graduate and take our places next to our fathers, Suco will step up as the leader on campus. I also heard one of my cousins would be attending that year as well, and he will be expected to help, just as previous generations have in the past. It's a constant cycle that turns through this university. The university that was built and founded by the early Dupree line and eventually became the home to The Illicit as they trained and made connections.

"How many years has it been since a Suco went through initiation at Delta Pi Theta?'

I glance at the pool table. "There haven't been any male Suco descendants since his father, eighteen years ago."

"Holy shit," Lee breathes out, "I knew my dad was always worried about their family, and always talked about how heavily this kid was guarded. Now it makes sense."

"If he's smart, the kid will come out swinging, ready to prove himself, and earn the top spot." I take my shot, instantly sinking the solid green ball.

"Guess we'll find out this semester," Lee replies, his eyes following my shot as I line up.

Lee is the next closest person to me after Soren, but I have to keep secrets even from him. In truth, I am worried about the Suco kid pledging this year. We have perfected a system that works for us, and Lee, Soren and myself ran the campus up until last year. Even though Bryce was around, we rarely kept company with him. Even back then, it was easy to see the type of lowlife he was, a parasite within our brotherhood. Lee and I have learned to cope with both Bryce and Soren gone and established another new normal. With the new freshmen coming in, sooner or later, I'll have to pull him deeper into the fold, and show him what it really means to be part of The Illicit. But that time isn't now.

"At least there won't be any other surprises. We knew eventually the Suco kid would be here. The Duprees are almost out; I think the old man is in his seventies. The Boudreaux family, on the other hand, hasn't even been heard from in almost twenty years," Lee adds.

I raise my brow. "Are you trying to jinx us or something? Don't let that shit out into the universe, man. The last thing we need is a long-lost family member showing up and splitting the empire even more."

"Or worse," Lee laughs, "they could be like the Van Dorens."

"I can't even think about it right now." I breathe out before taking another shot and hearing that satisfying sound of the cue ball knocking another solid into the pocket. Lee makes a strong point, though. What would we do if a Boudreaux member showed up?

Back in the day, when our fathers happened to be in the same graduating class, all six original members of The Illicit Brotherhood families had sons here that year. They had all been friends, according to the stories and murmurings I've heard over the years. Not only did they respect each other as colleagues, but they were close. No one is sure exactly what happened, but the fallout was that the Boudreaux member cut themselves off from the empire and hasn't been heard of since. Unfortunately, due to the founder's code, the family can't be replaced until they give up their spot formally, which requires blood. We're born in by lifeblood and let out by lifeblood.

We each take a few more shots, both of us lost in our own thoughts. It's only the start of September, yet it feels like we've been preparing for this all year.

"Hey, Carmichael!" Louie, one of the brothers in the house, peeks his head into the room. "Summer is here."

"Okay," I say, and he leaves right away. Blowing out a breath, I put my cue stick down and run my fingers through my hair. "Continue later?"

"Sure." Lee shrugs and puts his own cue stick back on the wall. "Have fun shopping." He smirks.

I lift both my middle fingers up as I back toward the door. "I'll make sure to pick out something for you."

Lee winces and shakes his head. "I'm good. Never again do I care if I celebrate Halloween."

I nod, the smile falling from my lips when the memory hits me. The noise of the splashing and the screaming. All the blood.

Hands down one of the worst parties we've ever thrown when it ends with an ambulance arriving and body parts missing. For some reason, Summer and the girls at our sister sorority are hellbent on still having the party, despite what happened last year. I don't particularly care about how Summer feels, but everyone keeps telling me that I should make my girlfriend happy, so we're having the party.

"Let's just stay out of the swamps this time, yeah?"

"That's dark." Lee laughs, shaking his head. He follows me out of the room and to the entry where Summer is waiting. Despite the drama the girl tends to create, I can't deny that she is amazing to look at. Tall, blonde, tan skin, and curves in all the right places. We met at the start of last year, right before the Halloween party. Her idea of *making me feel better* after the incident and Soren leaving was to wrap her lips around my cock. We started dating soon after.

"Baby!" she gushes, rushing over to me and throwing her body into mine. After a year together, I'm used to her over-enthusiastic greetings, and I push back the urge to cringe. Summer is a distraction, and I'm fully aware I wouldn't win any boyfriend of the year awards... I don't even know her last name, if I'm honest. I hear Lee snort behind me, but he quickly excuses himself and heads upstairs to where our rooms are located.

"You ready to go?" I ask Summer, stepping out of her embrace and giving us both breathing room.

"Yeah, baby." She flicks her hair over her shoulder. "I've been waiting."

I grab my keys, nodding and trying to make my face look remorseful. "Sorry, Lee and I had to finish up some business with the new pledges."

Sure enough, her eyes light up the minute I mention it. Summer and her sorority sisters live for pledge week. They've been planning for this year since the end of last year. I know way more about the hazing that goes on in sororities than I care to. I'm also convinced girls can be way more cruel in their process than we guys are. Complete a few drinking games, pull a few all-nighters, and the annual deep clean of the house is all that we require. The girls, on the other hand, get downright nasty.

"Our houses are still partnering up for the Tulle Ball, though, right?" she asks, and I nod my head yes, again. She smiles and grips my arm tightly as we leave the house.

Outside, a few of the guys are getting the float ready for the homecoming parade in two weeks. They nod at me as we leave, aware that I'm checking out their work. They know the float has to be big enough to hide that shipment of *gifts* my father plans to have delivered here. I lead Summer to my car, helping her get settled, before rounding to my side and getting in.

I listen to Summer talk the entire way to the mall, trying to remember to respond when it's appropriate. She keeps dropping hints about my tie. Delta Pi Theta brothers let others know when a relationship is serious by giving their partner their blue tie. It's an even bigger deal since very few have received the privilege. Summer wants it. *Badly.* But that's not my priority right now. My conversation with my father from earlier plays over and over in my mind. The little information he gave me about Soren fuels my anger once again. I made the only decision I could at the time, thinking I could keep him safe. Now he's across the ocean at some private location, only my father knows about, refusing to speak to anyone. I miss him, even though I'm not sure how things would be between us if he was here. Those shadows I often saw in him give me pause to think about how much worse last year could have been if he had stayed. It was better that he left, even if he didn't agree.

Eventually, we'll be together again.

For now, I'll take his hatred and silence.

CHAPTER TWO

Taylor

"I lost my virginity to a guy in a mask."

Why am I so awkward? I'm sitting criss-cross applesauce on my bed in my dorm room with my roommate, Ava. We've known each other for two months, and there's no doubt in my mind that she thinks I'm a total oddity. Actually, after that confession, all doubt has been erased. Ava knows she's rooming with a basket case.

She stares at me wide-eyed, as her mouth opens and closes several times. She appears horrified by my words. It *is* a strange way to experience your first time, I guess. "Are you...well, no— what I mean to ask is... Jesus, I'm so sorry, Taylor."

"Oh!" I can see where she misunderstood. That did come out all kinds of wrong. "Yeah, that sounds rapey, but it wasn't. I promise." Her eyebrows disappear behind her bangs. I fidget under her stare and rack my brain for something else to say. Then I remember how the police and EMTs had shown up that night. "It was a wild night, so much that a giant reptile bit a guy's leg off." *Are alligators reptiles?* "There must've been a full moon that night." *Why did I say reptile instead of alligator?*

Ava speaks slowly while watching me closely. "Must've been."

That's the only somewhat logical explanation I can come up with for how I behaved that night. Growing up in an extremely conservative household in a small town in the Bible Belt of the United States, I was sheltered when I arrived on the front steps of Thorn University, here in Blue Rose, Alabama. Not completely naïve, but I lacked life experience. Which is why I chose a university outside of Mississippi where I obtained a full-ride scholarship. Away from my overprotective family. I can only afford to visit on holidays, but we talk for one hour via video chat every Sunday night.

Last year, my sophomore year, I was tired of living like a nun. School, work, volunteer at the senior living center, church, repeat, that was my life. I'd never gone to any university social events. I've lived like a little mouse holed up in my room, only scurrying out to find food. I'd been terrified of everyone and everything up until that point. *Not saying that nuns live in fear, just that I did.* So I decided to attend a party and have at least one normal "college experience."

So how did I go from living like the Virgin Mary to being the girl who gets freaky with a guy in a mask? That's still kind of a mystery, since I didn't go to the frat party with the intention of losing my virginity that night. I only went with the intention of finally experiencing a college party. I love fall weather and dressing up, so that seemed like the perfect opportunity. Plus, hiding behind a costume gave me a little extra confidence. The decision to lose all sense of morals and reality hit me when I met *him.*

He'll have to be known only as 'him' because I never got his name.

Ava bursts out laughing. "Oh, girl. You bitch! You had me going. So, you and your boyfriend on Halloween... I get it now."

"Noooo," I draw the word out. "No boyfriend." *Definitely not.* My last boyfriend, only boyfriend, actually... I shake my head and force myself not to think about him. "He is what I like to refer to as my Masked V-Card Bandit."

"Wait...time-out. So, it was a hookup with some rando at a party? And why do you make it sound like you had sex with a raccoon? Masked bandit? Really?" She laughs.

"I don't know." It's shameful that I don't even know the guy's name or barely what he looked like, but I don't regret a single, sinful minute of it. It was my choice, and that's all that matters.

The only part I regret is how I handled it afterward. I'd gotten nervous and awkwardly shy. He went to the bathroom, and I'd told him I was going for a drink; I even offered to get him one as well. It must've taken too long for the drink, though, because he wasn't in the bedroom when I returned. I went in search of the masked crusader, but then the cops showed and everyone was scrambling to leave as soon as they could.

When I did find him, he was leaving the party with a gorgeous blonde.

Honestly, though, I'm not sure I expected anything different. I'd been warned how college and worldly guys are. He definitely proved that my parents were right on that account. Thankfully, they'll never be able to say *I told you so* because they'll never know about him. Even if I don't ever learn any more about him, at least I can say I'm no longer a virgin, and I did it my way.

"You look scared."

I jump from the low voice behind my back, spinning around and staring up into a looming figure in all-black, wearing a black hoodie with the hood up and a black mask with a blue neon-painted skull face. His sapphire eyes are as bright and as startling as the blue paint on the mask, a stark contrast against his dark attire. I think he even has black face paint around his eyes that make him look even more haunted.

Finding my courage, because I don't know him and he doesn't know me, I speak, "Two things. You were behind me." I hold up a finger and then raise a second one. "And I'm wearing sunglasses. At night. What makes you think I'm scared?"

I'm dressed as a blind mouse. I made the costume myself by putting together gray leggings, a white tutu, a gray shirt that reads, "I'm a Mouse, Duh," complete with a cute tail, pink bow tie, and a fur headband with ears. I added the sunglasses because, obviously, the three blind mice wore dark glasses. It also feels like an extra layer of protection since I'm painfully shy and sometimes looking people in the eyes makes me uncomfortable. Not to mention you can people-watch easier while wearing sunglasses because there's no awkward eye contact after getting caught. They never know. Am I looking at you, him, her—it's all a mystery. Tonight, I'm mysterious and interesting. My makeup is simple with a soft color lipstick, a pink nose, little black whiskers drawn on, and rosy cheeks. I'm the most covered person here by far. I feel like a middle school kid compared to all the sexy costumes that surround me. Then again, I think that was the last time I ever went to a Halloween party. In high school, my parents would only let me pass out candy for the little children who came by on Halloween. And even then, I had to dress up as a biblical character. Tonight, however, I'm out after nine at a fraternity bonfire party, dressed as a nursery rhyme character. How scandalous.

The masked face tilts to the side, sending an alarming chill down my spine as his eyes study me. Alarm bells are ringing in my head, but my heart is beating against my rib cage with excitement. There's something both terrifying and alluring about him. The aura of danger, the promise of a thrill, is what's making him so darn enticing. He's exactly what I've been missing out in life. Those eyes alone make me want to run away, yet at the same time crawl all over him while never looking away. I should go, but I'll never have an opportunity like this again. Pulling courage from my inner depths, something that shocks me to my core, I take a step into his space. I'm not sure what my next move is going to be, but I'm suddenly distracted because now I can see little blond eyebrow hairs. I wonder if I know him. What does he look like? Then again, anonymity is kind of nice. This is like my own little fairy tale. We dress up and can be whoever we want and pretend the other person is whoever we want. If I think about it, I have to ask if he's my Prince Charming or my very own big bad wolf.

He releases a low chuckle that's slightly muffled from the mask. "Tsk. Tsk. Be careful, Little Mouse." The masked stranger meets my challenge by stepping so close that our chests are barely a breath apart. "I'm a snake."

"Your costume isn't that convincing."

His head leans toward my ear. "How about I convince you another way? Do you know what snakes really love to eat? They devour little mice."

My chest barely brushes his as I try to control my breathing. What does he mean? He made it sound so dirty. The warmth of his hand on my side burns through the thin material of my shirt. His fingers flex ever so slightly and I find myself wanting to lean farther into his hand. I resist the urge and step back out of his grasp. Immediately, I regret the decision. Can I possibly grab his hand and place it back on my side? A part of me wonders what it would feel like to have that hand on my bare side.

"You have no clue who I am, do you?" He sounds surprised. "Do you even know where you are?" His voice carries a hint of amusement, which angers me. It's as if he's mocking me.

"I know where I am. I'm at a party, same as you. It's...Delta...Theta...fraternity." I think. I feel like I'm forgetting a letter from the Greek alphabet.

The party is carrying on around us while we stand there looking at each other. Me wearing sunglasses, not only indoors but at night like an idiot, and him in a full mask where I can't read his expression. This is great. The first college guy I really talk to and it's from behind a mask. Then again, maybe this is the only way I'm able to speak. I've been more outspoken these last ten minutes than I have since arriving at this school.

"You know any of these guys? From the Delta Theta...fraternity? Or maybe from the Delta Pi Theta one?"

He's playing with me. I wish I could see his stupid face. I bet he's laughing behind that ridiculous and creepy mask. I try to play it cool and coy.

"I now know you." I can feel myself beginning to sweat, so I do the worst thing possible; I keep talking. "Besides, you come to parties to meet people. You don't have to know everyone, it's a party. You make friends at parties. Maybe one of these people will be my new best friend, who knows."

Shut up. Shut up. Shut up. I sound so lame. Kill me now.

"Make friends? Is that why you came to the party?" His black-gloved hand reaches up. Ever so lightly, his fingertips touch the end of my shirt sleeve and then trail down my arm and to my fingertips. Chills follow in their wake, and I begin to feel my body tightening in new places. I can't answer him. My mouth has gone dry while other places are becoming increasingly wet. I stare at those aqua blue eyes surrounded by black paint and a mask, and I nod. I did come to make friends.

"I'll be your friend, Little Mouse."

Little Mouse. I guess that's to be my pet name now. That's the second time he's called me that, but this time, it was spoken like a term of endearment. His fingers entwine through mine, and he gives me a gentle tug. I follow him. Blindly, even. The irony of my costume is not lost on me. Turns out, it was more fitting than I could have ever imagined. A blind little mouse being led away by a snake.

I follow him through the massive house, which he seems to know well. He's either a part of the fraternity, or really good friends with whoever is. We enter a bedroom that only has a massive bed, a bookcase, and an elegant wooden desk with a lamp that's on. The desk is not fitting for a college student. This could be an office for a professor, aside from the huge, wooden four-poster bed.

We sit on the bed. He takes my hands in his black-gloved ones. I should be scared sitting here in a dimly lit room on a bed with a masked man. Every warning bell in my head should be sounding at the decibel level of deafness...but they aren't.

"Favorite genre of movies?"

"What?"

"What kind of movies do you like to watch?" he asks.

I lick my lips and then rub them together. I pop my lips and then make an unflattering 'um' sound before finally answering, "Romance. Romantic comedies."

"I like action and comedies, thanks for asking." I bite back a smile, and then mouth sorry. He continues, "Favorite books?"

"Romance..." I squint and release a nervous laugh. Quickly, I ask, "Yours?"

"Philosophy. Biographies." His hands begin massaging mine and moving up my wrists. "Hobbies?"

"Reading. Knitting. Singing. Your hobbies are?"

"Not knitting." I can hear the smile in his voice. I wish I could see it, but only the skull mask's static face looks back at me with those glowing blue eyes. "Photography. Martial arts."

Before he can ask me another question, I ask him, "Are you a student?"

"I am. Sophomore." He leans closer.

"Plans after college?"

"Go into the family business."

His hands release mine to remove my sunglasses. My chest rises and falls as his masked face inches closer to mine. The sinister skull with intense blue eyes giving nothing away. My throat feels thick, and my entire body is warm. We're silent as the room fills with a thick, heated tension.

What I realize is I'm not prepared for his strike. With mind-blowing speed, he raises the mask enough to expose perfectly-shaped lips that press against mine. I'm paralyzed against him. Just like a snake bite. His tongue slides into my mouth. My tongue is clumsy against his, but I enjoy the feel and taste of mint. I've kissed a boy before, but not like this. That boy was awkward and as nervous as me. Not this man. This masked stranger is confident, and with good reason. He obviously has more experience than I do, but honestly, it wouldn't take much for anyone to beat my experience level.

"If you don't want to go any further, stop me now. Tell me. Because I'm five seconds away from making you my meal." His voice is even more rich and smooth, without the mask hindering it.

I don't understand his words. Is this wordplay on my costume again? I look down and see his arousal. Yup. He's talking about sex. Do I really want this to be my first time? This isn't what good girls do. This isn't me. Making out with a stranger at a frat party. My first frat party, at that. Good Lord. But everything feels so good. My body is screaming to let him keep going.

"Are you hungry?" I cringe. Why would I say that? Why? That wasn't sexy. I shouldn't try to be coy or flirtatious; it doesn't work for me.

Yet his body begins to lean over mine, and his voice comes out lower. "I'm starving." A shiver goes through me. "Let's start with removing this." He pulls on the fluffy tutu, and I wiggle it down.

I lie back, laying my head on one of the thick pillows at the head of the bed. He straddles my waist, and the sight is so erotic. The lamp casting a glow behind him. His broad shoulders and height only emphasize his dark presence. I feel wetness between my legs as he holds his hands up and makes a show of slowly pulling each digit loose from the leather gloves. Once they're completely off, strong, long fingers are revealed. As his hand slides down my torso, toward my leggings, I notice a few cuts on his knuckles. Why am I finding that so sexy? It adds more to his bad boy and mysterious imagine. What if those are the hands of a total badass? A killer? What if I'm in bed with a modern-day James Dean, rebel without a cause? In reality, he probably just has dry skin and the most rebellious thing he does is not moisturize.

He toys with the band of my leggings, and I realize where he's going. Panic settles in the pit of my stomach. He'll feel how wet I am. Embarrassment and insecurities have my voice coming out way louder than intended. "Wait!"

The hand that's barely inside my leggings immediately halts its journey. "What's wrong? I mean, I'll stop if you want."

I gulp so loud, there's no way he missed it. I stare up at the ceiling, trying to figure out what to say. Tears begin to build behind my eyes. I need my sunglasses back. I close my eyes to hide the truth from him, but a traitorous tear slides down.

"Hey, what's wrong? We don't have to do anything." His voice has turned so gentle.

"Something is wrong. I'm, oh God, this is so humiliating."

"Tell me. It's okay, I promise."

"I feel really...like...really wet down there. I don't know. I know it's normal to get a little...but I'm afraid to think about what if I accidently peed? Or if I have an infection? It's just that my panties are soaked."

Stop talking. Stop talking, Taylor. Did you seriously just tell a guy, who has his hand down your pants, you might have peed yourself or have some type of an infection? My gosh. It's a wonder I didn't go ahead and blurt out I'm worried it smells.

I practice good hygiene, but for some reason, in this very moment, I'm terrified of the condition of my vagina. That's it, I never need to leave the house. I don't need to be part of society. I clearly have no social or seductive skills whatsoever.

"Let me check." He barely gets the words out as his hand eases under my panties. Something between a groan and laugh escapes him. "Believe me, there's nothing wrong. And to prove it..." he says as he rises up and begins to pull my leggings and panties down. Through the darkness, I can make out the white of his teeth. I bet he does have a killer smile. Just like the kiss to my lips earlier, I'm not prepared for the delivery of the next kiss. Because his mouth lands somewhere I never imagined I'd be kissed.

I'm reminded again of how he referred to himself as a snake. His tongue is doing wicked things to my body. My thighs tighten against his head, and my hand reaches down to touch the hoodie that's covering his hair. I tug it back to discover his hair is longer than I thought it'd be. I grab a fistful of soft locks to hold him to me.

"Okay, you can stop." I moan. "I'm not sure I can handle any more." My body feels on the verge of exploding. He doesn't stop, but instead nips me, sending a sensation unlike any other I've felt through my body. "Or don't. Actually, don't stop."

I feel him smile against me, and when he speaks, the feel of his breath again my most sensitive area has me trembling beneath his hold. "You like that?"

"I do. Yeah, I mean. You could do it again..."

And he does. And he does more. I'm wound so tight that when he inserts two fingers inside me, I explode. I hold him so tightly against me that there's no way he can breathe. I cry out, and my body rubs against his face as the waves take over.

As soon as my body stills, he's on top of me. The mask is gone, but his face is still mostly disguised by black paint around his eyes and smudges along his cheeks.

Our clothes are being ripped off with frantic hands. He sits on his heels and then brings a foil packet to his mouth. He rips it open with his teeth, and then pulls out a condom. I watch as his sure and quick fingers roll the condom down his shaft.

Our teeth clack as our mouths join. I'm met next with a quick jolt of pain between my legs. I suck in a mouthful of air from the shock. His mouth covers mine, claiming my gasps as his hips start to thrust inside me, over and over again, the pain fading, but still there, as my body adjusts. My arms and legs lock around his strong torso, anchoring him to me. He pulls his mouth back, and our eyes lock, before he drops a chaste kiss on my lips, and then my cheek. He trails down my neck with those same kisses, and when he reaches my collarbone, the tip of his warm tongue traces the delicate skin along the bone. He flattens his tongue and licks up my neck, all the way to my earlobe, where he sucks my flesh into his mouth, and then I feel the pinch of his teeth. I moan obscenely loud and I'm thankful that we're locked away from the rest of the party, so no one can hear me.

His strong hand grips my hair, almost painfully. I cry out, and his voice is right there in my ear. "Oh, Little Mouse," he sighs, "you are so fucking sweet." He groans into my neck as he adds more force behind each thrust. "You feel incredible."

I can't even respond. My entire body is on fire. There's a stretching ache between my thighs from his rough movements that is an uncomfortable and foreign feeling, along with the sensation of his warm body against mine, and his tender kisses.

"I'm not going to be able to last. I want to do this all night, but dammit...you feel so fucking good, I can't." He rises up and his eyebrows pinch together. I stare up into his face, that is partly shadowed from the dim lighting, and it's twisted in a look of pure ecstasy and pain. His lean, muscled arm twitches as he supports his weight above me. "Tell me you're almost there."

There? He must read my expression through the darkness because he makes a slight 'hmmm' sound. His hand appears in front of his face, and he spits on the tips of his fingers. I'm so confused as to why, until I feel those lubed fingers slowly massage my clit, working it around in a circular motion. My body tightens so much I could snap. Those fingers begin moving faster. My skin is too sensitive. I don't think I can handle much more. It almost hurts. But I want more. I need more. He adds more pressure with his fingers and in his rapid movements. Finally, he presses against me hard with his thumb, and I gasp from the shock of intense pleasure. My body begins to move against him, with him—honestly, I'm not sure. All I know is there's this passion and fire running through me, and he is my sole focus. He is the cause of everything I'm feeling in this moment. At some point, my eyes must've shut, because I open them to see the face of what could only be described as an angel of death. He's simply beautiful.

I'm lost in his beauty when he suddenly pulls out, causing minor discomfort. Before I have time to react, he rips the condom off and then his body leans over mine, his hand fisting around his cock as he thrusts three more times. I watch as warm, thick liquid lands in ropes along my collarbone. I'm completely stunned. The urge to reach up and touch it is strong, but I force my hands to remain on him as a satisfied smirk crosses his face.

He reaches over and opens the drawer on the nightstand next to the bed. He pulls out an old camera. "May I?"

"I'm not sure..."

"This camera uses film. And you look too stunning not to photograph right now." When I don't respond he says, "Nobody will ever see it. It'll only be for me."

I don't know him. Hell, I don't even know his name. For whatever reason, probably the fact that I'm insane, I slowly nod, granting him permission. There's a long flash and then a click.

"Fucking beautiful."

I want to ask him if he does this with all the girls he sleeps with, but I don't. However, the thought must be transparent because he leans down and whispers, "No. You're the only one I've used my camera on. Photography is my passion. I don't like to waste film."

He gets out of bed and then returns with a warm cloth. He's completely at ease while cleaning me up, while I'm trying to figure out how I'm supposed to act now.

"You didn't come."

"What?" I ask him.

"You didn't orgasm. There might've been a mini one, but I couldn't hold it any longer."

Without thinking, I blurt out, "A mini is better than nothing. I didn't hate it."

He releases a short chuckle, and I love the sound. I truly didn't hate it, though. I enjoyed the feel of him holding me, his strong yet gentle fingers sending tingles everywhere they touched, the little sounds he made, the intensity of his eyes, and his open mouth kisses worshipping my body.

"You didn't hate it," he repeats. "Well, Little Mouse," his voice turns darker, "I'll admit I wasn't prepared for you. Now I am. Because I didn't hate it either—far from it." I can hear the smile in his voice when he says, "I only hate that I didn't give you the best night of your life."

He has no idea how much this night means to me. How this night compares to my others. Even if I didn't get a mind-blowing orgasm, he still made my body feel things I never thought possible. "But you did."

His rough knuckle caresses my cheekbone. "Oh, sweet Little Mouse. Just wait. Just wait for the plans I have for you."

I wave bye to Ava, feeling foolish having shared my deepest and darkest truth. A secret I've held on to for almost a year. A one-night stand that changed my life and awakened a part of myself I'd been scared of for far too long. She told me at least it proves I'm not completely boring. If it wasn't so true, I'd be insulted by that remark. Ava didn't judge me, and that is why I know our friendship will stand the test of time. I haven't seen my masked bandit since that night. It's like he disappeared from campus. Even when I admitted to her that I spent months looking for what I knew of his face in the crowded hallways or in the quad, Ava didn't bat an eye. She accepts my crazy.

What I didn't share was my pitiful and sordid past. The relationship that drove me out of my hometown. The one that finally caused a divide between me and my parents. It's what was behind my determination to lose the one thing that my ex was obsessed over. I feel a small satisfaction that I gave it to a nameless face. And now that it's gone, hopefully, when or if I do decide to return home, *he'll* have moved on and be gone too. I refuse to even think or say his name. Mama always said a person's name is all they have, and it's what holds power. She always said we determine how much control a person holds over us, being angry gives that person power; it's another sense of manipulation—of influence—they have. I've brought peace to myself by physically escaping him and eliminating his name from my mind. I'll continue enjoying my new life here, which is going pretty well.

I landed my dream job at the university library. The scholarship program and financial aid office helped me obtain the position, and it honestly couldn't be any more perfect. It's quiet; I don't have to interact with people much, and I can also read and work on my studies when my duties are done.

I greet people as I walk around to my station at the front desk. Dropping my backpack down on the floor, I login to the computer and clock in, getting cozy in my seat and preparing for an uneventful and easy shift.

About an hour into it, the front door opens, and I glance up from my paper. The guy who walks through has my heart jumping into my throat and completely leaving my body. Seriously. I'm dead. My heart has been ripped out of my body completely because that can't be...

I'd recognize that chiseled jawline anywhere. Those perfectly-shaped lips. It was dark that night, but his stark features could never be mistaken. The way he walks with confidence and authority. I wish I could see his eyes. But he doesn't even notice me. Why would he? I'm over here behind a huge desk, hunkering down. I quickly ease out of my chair, because I have to know if it's him. On light feet, I trail down the aisle, following after him. He goes to the very back of the library, so I hurry down the one next to him. Peeking between the books and shelves to watch him, I continue following. He stops and looks around. Can he sense me?

I'm floored when I get a look at his eyes. *It's him.* My Masked V-Card Bandit. I want to stare into those gorgeous, steel blue eyes again. Beg him to make eye contact with me, to recognize me. To remember me and our night. But I avert my eyes and pretend to walk away. When I hear the sound of him walking again, I spin around and tiptoe after him.

My heart plummets when he stops. I peek through the shelves again and see a gorgeous blonde waiting for him. She wraps her arms around him. I should look away, but I don't. I watch as he does to her what I've fantasized him doing to me again for almost a year now.

"It was him!" I shout as I pace our dorm room.

"Are you sure? To be fair, it happened a year ago, and he was in makeup. Wasn't he painted like a raccoon?" Ava sits on the edge of her bed with one foot propped as she paints her toenails.

"No," I grit my teeth, "but I would recognize those eyes anywhere. His height. The hair. Those lips...*God*. Those lips."

"Why didn't you catch him as he was leaving?"

"You mean, wait for him to finish, and then stand by the door and ask him how it was?"

"Were you thinking about asking for seconds instead?" she questions before blowing on her toes.

"You're gross."

"This is a huge campus. Most likely, like the past almost twelve months, you won't see him again."

"Unless he comes to the library."

"Maybe he'll check out a book and you'll finally learn his name."

"That's not a bad idea, but the thought of facing him is humiliating. I'm ninety percent certain that was the girl he left me for at the party."

"Then hopefully you won't ever have to see that dick again."

Yeah, hopefully. A big part of me can't stop thinking about said dick and would like to see it, again. Oh, geez. He's turned me into a harlot. A veritable biblical outcast. Ava begins laughing at me. I make a pouty face and she makes one back at me. "Come over here. Sit." She pats her bed. "Let me paint your nails while we chat. Getting pampered always lightens my mood. Come on. It might make you feel better."

I don't see how, but it certainly won't make me feel any worse. In a rather dramatic manner, I flop onto Ava's bed and stick my foot out to her. She begins to paint my big toe, and then asks, "Have you told your parents you're switching majors? That you don't want to be a minister?"

"Yes. They're not happy."

They're also not happy I refuse to speak to *him*. I won't come home. They really would lose their minds if they knew all I've done. Changing my major is the least of my sins and grievances.

Luckily, it's still early in the semester, so I can easily get started on my new major—psychology. The next day, I enter my first class, Intro to Psychology, with high hopes. As I'm walking to an empty desk, my heart slams against my rib cage as I meet glacier blue eyes. My foot trips over something, sending me to the ground.

"Hey, are you okay?"

No. No, I'm really not.

CHAPTER THREE

Steffan

I'm used to girls falling at my feet, figuratively, but this might be the first time it's happened *literally*. The poor girl looks like she can't decide if she wants to laugh or cry. I'm hoping for the former Girls and tears have never really been my thing, unless they're in my bed and they're tears of joy. I run my eyes over her hands and knees quickly, to make sure there are no injuries, then head back up to her face. When her deep, coffee eyes meet mine, I'm surprised to see the flare of anger there. Deciding to go easy on her, I reach my hand down and grab her elbow, helping her stand.

"You okay?" I ask again, once she's on her feet. I easily tower over her, and she has to tilt her head back when she finally looks at me.

"I'm fine," she retorts with mock pleasantries, and I have to resist the urge to laugh. This girl is hardly over five feet, and while it looks like she might have curves in all the right places, I could probably knock her out with a feather. She is not a threat, but I do like the fierceness she is exuding.

"I'm Steffan," I tell her. She looks slightly familiar, but she's not from any of the sororities. I would know. Thanks to dating Summer, the frat has been invited to all the sorority mixers.

Her dark brow arches. "Oh, we're exchanging names this time?" Her voice is laced with sarcasm, and again, I have to stifle my laugh. Feisty Girl yanks her elbow out of my hand and shuffles her way around me. I watch her as she glances around the room, finding that all the other seats are already taken except for one. The seat right next to mine. Her cheeks flush pink as she ducks her head and quickly sits down. Our professor enters the room next, and I make a move to sit back where I was. The second I do, her scent engulfs me. Vanilla and sugar. Sweet. Natural. Intoxicating. Her shoulders stiffen when she realizes I'm still watching her.

"Do I know you?"

A small, nervous laugh escapes her lips, and her cheeks get pinker. "Are you being serious right now?"

My eyes narrow. I've clearly hit a nerve with this girl, only I can't remember exactly what I did. Usually our business doesn't involve females, and with Summer around, I've been able to put off the crushes, stalkers, and fainters who followed me around. Even as a member of Delta Pi Theta, I don't go out of my way to be rude to women, but once in a while, I just don't have the time to listen to pitches for a fundraiser, or to stop and take a picture for the next charity event that is being held by a campus club. I'd recognize her if I had, though. She's beautiful, but not in a plastic and made-up way. She would have stuck out among the other students.

Our professor starts explaining our first assignment, but I keep my eyes on my new tablemate. Awareness tickles the back of my brain, a face, lips parted in shock, but I can't pull the memory fully forward.

"Taylor Mae Lake?" Professor Brooks calls. Feisty Girl lifts her hand slowly, while trying to keep her face hidden with her long curtain of dark brown hair.

"You and...Steffan Carmichael?" The professor points at me, while getting confirmation on my name.

"Present," I reply easily, while the professor writes our names down on his paper, making us partners for the whole semester.

I finally have a name. "Taylor Mae, huh?"

She glances at me sideways and rolls her eyes. "Just Taylor."

This girl is sassy. My smirk grows wider. "Okay, Just Taylor, are you going to tell me how you know me?"

I hear her intake of breath, and she glances at me again, this time a trace of fear skating across her face, and I feel my body respond to it. "You aren't a sorority sister."

She scoffs. "No." Fair enough. The Greek life isn't for everyone. The only reason I participate is that it gives our brotherhood the perfect cover. Fraternity life provides a large enough house for all of us, the security of a campus setting, and enough activities on campus and around town for us to participate in that makes moving guns, ammunition, and/or drugs easier to do. It's the perfect cover.

"Were you at McGyer's party last weekend?"

"I haven't been to a party in almost a year." Taylor turns her body toward mine.

"Chewy's?" I throw out, thinking it has to have been there. It's the most popular restaurant near campus. On game days, it's the go-to for pregaming, and it reverts to a nightclub on weekend evenings.

"Why do you care?"

"I don't." I shrug, letting the lie roll off my tongue easily. I actually don't know why I care, though. If I can't remember her, then our encounter must not have been that memorable in the first place.

Taylor huffs and turns back to the front where the professor is now going over the syllabus for the year.

"Half of your grade will depend on your ability to work with your small groups and by choosing one psychological myth to present to the class. Thirty percent will go toward the data and findings from your research, and the last twenty percent will be taken from your midterm quiz and final exam."

I hate group projects. I hate having to rely on anyone who isn't part of my family or the brotherhood, and fifty percent of a grade is a lot of faith to put into someone else's commitment.

"We're going to start with a warm-up exercise today, and next week, I will assign groups. Please turn to the person next to you, and go over these questions," Professor Brooks instructs while starting to write as he starts writing on the board. "You will say the first word that comes to your mind after your partner asks the question."

I turn to Taylor, only to find that she is already watching me. My lip kicks up again when I see the irritated look she is giving me. "So, Taylor," I roll her name around on my tongue and watch her fingers grip her laptop tighter. "Favor—"

"Halloween."

My hackles instantly rise, since I didn't even get the full word out, and I feel my gut clench. That's her favorite holiday? Fuck Halloween. After last year, and all the shit we went through, I may never think of the holiday the same. My eyes scan her face and notice the hardness in her stare, before her gaze narrows, almost accusingly. Was she there? Shit. Did she see? Her words from earlier come back to me.

I search my brain, trying to remember her. It's in there somewhere. I know that I've seen her, the dark hair framing her face, her chocolatey eyes widening, and those rose petal pink lips parting in surprise. My memory is foggy, but did she have something in her hands? I run through the whole night from last year. Getting to the party, Summer, the phone call, the fight, Bryce. The alligator. Sending my brother away. Sirens, lots of blood and more phone calls. Summer. Wait...

My eyes snap back to hers as she says on her turn, "Favorite..."

"The library."

Taylor huffs, that pink flush creeping down her neck now. "The library isn't a school subject."

"No," I snap my fingers, "that's where I know you. You work at the library."

It all comes back to me right then. Taylor watching, while I railed Summer in the stacks. I saw her, and instead of stopping, I kept going. Summer didn't notice, and Taylor hadn't stuck around long after we made eye contact, anyway. I know I must have it right when Taylor's mouth drops open. Anger flashes in her eyes, and I can't stop the rumble of laughter in my chest.

"You're unbelievable," she grits through her teeth.

"Me?" I laugh again. "Did you get yourself off while I was getting my girlfriend off?"

Taylor's face hardens, and she jumps to her feet right as the class is ending. Practically running out of the room, she brushes past me. I ignore the way my skin tingles from where her body touched mine. My gaze tracks her the whole way, and I fight the urge to follow her into the hallway. Taylor Mae intrigues me, and it's more than her voyeurism adventure, which was hot as hell. Might have been the sass she was throwing, or the way she didn't seem to care about the reputation that precedes me. I think this psych class might just be my new favorite subject.

"And she ran?" Lee laughs, hitting me on the back, before lining up to hit the ball into the pocket.

"Like her ass was on fire," I confirm and bite the inside of my cheek to keep the grin off my lips. "It's a nice ass, though."

"Better not let Summer hear you say that," Lee warns, shaking his head. "I think she has wedding bells in mind."

I shake my head. "Summer is a good time. Plus, her sorority working with Delta Pi Theta helps us with most of our covers and alibis."

"Is she tie-worthy, though?" Lee asks, and I meet his eyes before glancing at the next ball I plan to sink into the pocket.

"No," I answer easily, with no hesitation. Giving a woman a blue tie in our organization is the equivalent to handing over a diamond ring. A symbol of our undying devotion and their place in our life. Metaphorically tying them to us. It's a commitment, and with the life I live in the brotherhood, with my position of power, it will take more than just love for me to give up my tie. To any woman.

I'm so deep in thought that I miss the knock at the door. "Someone better be dead." Lee groans as he walks over to the door and opens it.

"What, Scab?" he calls to one of the new pledges, who is almost cowering in the hallway.

"I, uh," he swallows, "it's about one of the brothers. He's been saying some things about the females on campus. I think something bad is going to happen, or it already did."

My brow rises and I walk around the pool table, leaning against it. "This is something you saw?"

"No, I heard it." He manages to get the words out, his hands fisted at his sides. I run my gaze over the new pledge, remembering his file. Charlie Maccon. Eighteen. From Boise, Idaho. Hates spiders and is allergic to shellfish. His family is connected to the Blood Disciples, a powerful MC that we buy and sell firearms to.

"What did you hear?"

"He was bragging about this girl from the party on Saturday. She turned him down and he said he had something that would change her mind. Said she would be too out of it to reject him while he taught her a lesson," Charlie explains.

I glance at Lee, whose eyes are narrowed on Charlie. "Didn't take you for a snitch, Maccon."

My eyes slide to Charlie, his face turning red. "Why are you telling us, Scab?"

"Because Delta Pi Theta doesn't hurt women, right? We don't trade skin, and we keep all our business out of strip clubs. We don't even wash money through massage parlors, so I thought this would be something you'd be against. Besides, if he was a real man, he wouldn't need whatever he is talking about to get a girl to sleep with him. He would take the rejection and move on."

I study him, slightly impressed with his knowledge of the brotherhood's businesses, but even more so with his regard for women. His little speech gives me insight into how he views them, which aligns with our beliefs as well. "Did anyone else hear this?"

He nods. "A few of the guys in the arcade."

I glance at Lee, who is already waiting for my instructions. If no one can corroborate Charlie's story, then it will be bad for him and my hands will be tied. "Who is it?"

"One of the other pledges, Tommy Locke."

Fuck. The Locke family has been a thorn in my side for the past two years. They knew their son would be here eventually, and Mr. Locke has used every opportunity at his disposal to kiss ass. The only reason I play nice is because Mr. Locke happens to be the second-in-command of one of the most powerful cocaine dealers in Louisiana.

"That's going to be a problem," Lee agrees with my silent inner turmoil.

We need someone with more credit than just a few of the other Scabs in order to get our point across. Anything less and it could be a problem with our southern distribution, which is never good for business. "Call Suco in here."

Lee's brow rises, but he keeps his thoughts to himself. Charlie moves out of the way as Lee passes him. I notice for the first time that Charlie's skin tone is returning to normal, but there is still some wariness in his gaze.

"You do realize that threatening rape is heavily punished here," I ask.

"Yes, sir," Charlie answers, his Adam's apple bobbing in his throat.

I slide my hands into my pockets and wait. After a few more minutes, Lee walks in with Jose Suco, and another pledge, Nathaniel. "Carmichael."

I nod my head, before glancing at Charlie, who has also stepped farther into the room. "I heard something interesting about Locke."

Nathaniel glances at Jose. Interesting. "Locke is an important pawn on the board," Jose answers.

"Doesn't matter," I shrug, "I've killed people for less. You know the rules, you learned the code."

"What are you asking, then?" Jose glances between Lee and me.

"Is it true?" I spread my hands out, then hop off the table and stand in front of him. "If you can't corroborate the story, then he walks. If you can, then we deal with it."

Suco looks from Charlie to Nathaniel before glancing back at me. "He plans to use a new formula that his family created. All the same effects, except for hours of memory loss, so the victim feels as if she really only did get wasted. Shit's even untraceable in a blood draw."

"You knew about this?" Lee asks, a hard edge to his voice.

"We've been paying attention to the distribution. It hasn't reached him yet, and we know it is not on campus. If it had gotten here, we'd have let you know. With my position, you know I can't be a rat, Concord," Jose talks it through, and I hate that he's right. In the end, though, it's settled.

"Call a meeting," I instruct Lee, and soon, his phone is to his ear.

Half an hour later, I've read all the material on what I now know is Project Ladybug, a nod to the coloring of the little pill, and I've made my father aware of the situation. He discussed it with the brotherhood, and I have the authority to dole out the necessary punishment.

A crowd has gathered in the basement by the time we're ready. Tommy Locke is front and center. I notice the fear he is trying to mask under his cocky smirk. I pocket my knife and head down into the room. The talking becomes a whisper, and soon that fades away when I step into the light, my anger and disgust no longer hidden in the shadows on my face.

"Locke." Lee motions the guy forward. He looks like he's about to piss his pants. I cock my head to the side and glance over him for any evidence of weapons on him. I see none and incline my head for Lee to continue.

"What's this about?" Tommy asks, chuckling, but there is an edge of nervousness in his tone.

"Project Ladybug," Lee answers for me. Tommy's face turns pale, and the room erupts into whispers. "The thing is, Locke, you're in Blue Rose. On our turf. At T.U. A pledge of Delta Pi Theta. You belong to The Illicit Brotherhood until graduation. Any other member and pledge here tonight can tell you," Lee turns to the crowd, "WHAT IS OUR CODE ON RAPE?"

"MEN DON'T RAPE, SIR. THE OFFENSE IS PUNISHABLE BY DEATH, SIR," the whole crowd chants, sure and strong.

"I didn't rape anyone!" Tommy steps back, his hands in the air.

"Last Saturday, a co-ed turned down your advances, Locke. I heard you've been a busy bee telling everyone what you were going to do to her, the minute you could get some of your dad's new product into her, against her will," Lee explains. "That's pre-meditated sexual assault. A crime in any state. Too bad for you, you're held to The Illicit Brotherhood's standards—not the local sheriff's department—for how we handle sex crimes."

"You dug your own grave, Tommy boy," I finally speak and watch as the sweat beads on his forehead. His skin turns sickly green.

"You can't kill me," he sneers, "it would mean a war and you know it!"

I keep my eyes on Locke, but signal with a nod of my head for them to take him. "Maybe. But no one said anything about killing you, did we?"

Two of our senior brothers rush Locke, grabbing his arms and dragging him to the altar. He's pushed into a chair, his legs strapped and arms tied down. He keeps struggling, swearing, trying to knock away anyone who comes near him. A smile curls my lips, and I slip my hand back into my pocket, grab my blade and pull it out. The noise in the room dies down, and everything stills. I touch my fingertip to the edge of the blade and stalk across the space toward Tommy. His eyes widen when he sees the weapon in my hand. He has no fucking idea what's in store for him.

I nod at Lee, who's able to get an arm around Locke's head. My hand reaches out, gripping his jaw and forcing his lips apart. He screams, and it's with that momentum, I'm able to slide my blade in and cut through the fleshy part of his tongue. My hand comes back bloody, leaving a strand of blood and spit dangling from his mouth to my hand. Sweat covers his chest, and his skin turns pale. I grab the front of his hair, pulling his head up so he can see me. "I can't kill you, but the great thing is, you can live without your tongue. Never again will you speak of women that way." Locke makes a choking noise, and more tears fall from his eyes. I have zero remorse for rapists. In my opinion, a bullet to the head would have been better. Now, Tommy's father will have to decide what to do with him. Brotherhood justice was served.

The room becomes frenzied, but I'm already on my way out, Lee at my back. I leave the seniors to move Locke, and the Scabs to clean up the mess. Right at the steps, I spot Suco in the back. He dips his head in respect, and I nod in return. I could get used to the kid being around. He proved himself with his knowledge and loyalty tonight. Both of which make him a perfect fit for The Illicit.

CHAPTER FOUR

Taylor

Such a jerk face! I'm still fuming over Steffan. Ugh. *Steffan.* What a stupid name. Actually, it's not. It's the right amount of mystery and hotness. It fits him. Which makes everything worse! Even his name is sexy. He saw me watching him have sex, but he doesn't remember having sex with me. I'm not sure if things could get any more bizarre or humiliating.

"Hey!" a voice calls out. "*Hey!* Girl who tripped in class!" That would be me. I'm now known as *the girl who tripped in class.* I stop walking and spin around.

"I'm assuming you mean me, unless there's someone else who is having a bad day?"

"Bad day, huh? Well, would a new friend make the day better? A new friend who buys you coffee?"

I stand there and blink at this person, who appeared out of nowhere, offering to buy me a hot beverage. She's extremely beautiful with legs for days and long, shiny light copper hair. Her eyes are insanely round and brown, sparkling with happiness. If I've learned anything from fairy tales and my love for musicals and animated movies, it's that bad people don't have glittering eyes, so that's a good sign. At least she's not a mean girl coming to further humiliate me.

"What's the catch?" I look around for a hidden camera crew or something. "Is this some kind of reality show? Is it a joke? I don't understand."

"No. I'm not fucking with you." She laughs. "I'm offering to buy you a drink."

Realization sets in, and I smile widely at her. "Wow. I'm flattered, honestly, because you're crazy hot. This would actually be amazing for me, you're kind of lowering the bar for yourself, though, because you're so out of my league. However, I'm not into women. But I really appreciate it. This really helped boost my ego and, God, did I need it."

"Oh my gosh. You're a riot. Can we be best friends, like now?" She's laughing and shaking her head at me.

"I'm confused."

"You don't make a lot of friends, do you? I'm not fucking *with* you or trying *to* fuck you. I'm not offering to buy you a drink as in asking you out. I ride dick, too. I'm legit inviting you to walk with me to the café." She points across the street. "That one right there."

"But why?"

"Because you fell on your ass in class yesterday. So, I thought, I'm going to buy that clumsy bitch a coffee."

"Okay."

We're just crossing the street when a thought dawns on me. I stop in the middle of the crosswalk. My new friend, who is determined to buy me a coffee, stops as well. She looks around and then back to me with furrowed brows.

I extend my hand and say, "I'm Taylor. What's your name?"

"You are a trip." She laughs. "I'm Kali Jones. Did we really need to stop traffic for introductions? I was just going to wait and listen for what name they used to call for your coffee."

I laugh. She's funny and outgoing. I like her, so I give her the best answer I can. "It's just that I have a really bad habit of not getting people's names. And I didn't want to make that mistake again."

As I walk back to my dorm room, I feel lighter. I have a new friend. Kali is a sophomore, but this is her first year at Thorn University. She told me she was nervous leaving her mom back in Louisiana because it's always been just the two of them. She never had a personal relationship with her father. In fact, she only learned of his existence by snooping through her mother's financial records. He'd been supporting them all her life, so she assumed he must somewhat care for her. However, after she reached out to him, he went ballistic on her mother for revealing his identity. Kali told me her goal in life now is to become wealthier and more powerful than he ever thought possible. *It's good to have goals, even if they're vengeful ones, I guess.* She can't stand her roommate and is living in one of the older dorm buildings, but hoping she can find a resident advisor position next year, so she'll get a private room.

As I walk into our room, Ava greets me. "How was class?"

"His name is Steffan."

"You found him?" Ava turns in her chair, away from her computer, and gives me her full attention.

"Yes. He's in my psychology class and I sit next to him. And, Ava, he doesn't remember me."

She stands up and rushes over to me. I didn't realize how much I needed a hug until I feel her arms wrap around me. A calm settles over me. It's nice to be comforted.

"Want pizza?" she asks as her arms release me.

"Can I get pineapple on half?"

She speaks in a sarcastic tone, one I do not appreciate, as she walks back to her desk to pick up her phone. "I don't know what's more shocking. You eating pineapple on pizza, or finding out you lost your virginity to a masked frat guy named Steffan?"

"It's more common than you think!"

"The frightening part is I'm not sure which one you're referring to..."

I frown at her, but she only smirks at me. Ava calls our pizza in, and about thirty minutes later, they call back letting us know they're downstairs waiting.

Ava and I go down together and stop at the vending machine for a couple of sodas. She's holding the pizza, while I'm inserting change into the vending machine...and that's when I hear it. A low chuckle, followed by a deep voice saying, "You've got to be kidding me."

I turn around to see Steffan and another guy. They begin walking toward us, and I'm so flustered that when the soda drops into the bin behind me, I drop the can I'm holding. It falls with a loud pop as Coke spews everywhere.

"Shit!" Ava cries.

Steffan and the other guy double over in laughter. When the carbonated bomb finally settles, they finish their approach. "I come in peace. Don't fire another one at us, all right?"

A few choice words come to mind, but I bite my tongue. I turn around and focus on getting another soda.

"Hi, I'm Steffan," he says to Ava. "Taylor's...*friend?*"

Her mouth drops open. "I'm Ava. I'm also her friend and roommate."

"We're also partners. In class, anyway." Steffan adds and then turns and winks. He actually winks at me, the freakin' blockhead. He jerks his thumb toward his friend. "This is Lee. He's my housemate and brother."

"Like blood brother or frat brother?" Ava asks.

"I'd say we're blood brothers more than frat brothers, but we're not biologically related."

I can't stop myself when I mumble, "That doesn't make any sense and sounds so stupid."

My skin is burning from the heat coming from his eyes. He brings his mouth to my ear, and in a deadly calm voice, he whispers, "You don't agree or understand something, so you think it's stupid. That sounds a bit narrow-minded. I gave you too much credit. I thought you were smarter. I'll need to find a new partner. I can't risk my GPA."

"You'd be doing me a huge favor," I reply.

When he remains silent, I turn my head. That was a mistake because now our lips are too close together. The scent of mint is intoxicating. Up close I can see there are multiple shades of blue in his eyes. Sapphire. Turquoise. A hint of gray. They're stunning. He's gorgeous. However, his smug, crooked smile makes me want to drop to my knees at his feet as well as throat punch him. Can he tell I'm attracted to him? Of course, he can.

"This is going to be so much fun." He reaches around me and presses a button. I frown at the sound of the machine dispensing another drink because that's my money he's using.

Steffan grabs the can and pops the top. Then he walks over to Ava and lifts the pizza lid. He and Lee each help themselves to a slice and then walk away.

"Hey!" I yell.

"See you Wednesday," he calls, without bothering to spare me another glance. I stare through the glass as he exits the building and crosses the parking lot.

I turn to Ava and throw my hands up. "Why did you let them take off with two slices of our pizza?"

"Why'd you let him take your soda?"

"I didn't want that flavor, so why fight for it?"

Ava smirks at me and raises one shoulder. "I didn't want pineapple, so I didn't fight them over it."

"He took mine?" I whine.

Before I can throw a total temper tantrum, a male voice cuts in. "Excuse me?"

I turn around to see an attractive guy with dark red hair and a dimple in his cheek. "I'm sorry, excuse me." I step out of his way to the vending machine. It's then that I notice he has a slight limp, something more pronounced than a sprained ankle, it appears from the way he centers his body weight. But then he speaks and I'm momentarily distracted.

"Yum. That pizza smells amazing."

I scoff. "Help yourself to a slice. Everyone else is." When he turns to stare at me, I quickly apologize. "I'm sorry. That was rude. We just had some real charmers come by."

"Sorry. Let me apologize on behalf of jerks everywhere."

Ava giggles and I turn to study her. She's blushing. I smile and look back at the guy. He is cute. "Thank you. Well, if you don't have dinner plans, we could eat in the lobby?" I smile as Ava stares wide-eyed at me. "Or go out on the terrace?"

I look back at Ava, both of us fighting back smiles.

"Sure. That'd be great." He throws us a friendly nod and grins. "By the way, my name is Bryce Van Doren."

I spend the next two weeks trying my best to ignore Steffan during our psychology class that meets Mondays and Wednesdays. Twice a week. That's three hours every week. He also comes into the library. And like clockwork, shortly after Summer walks in, they go have sex in the back. I may or may not watch. Again. *God, I've really turned into a pervert since coming here.* Every day here I have to pray for my soul a little harder. I've gone to saying my prayers three—sometimes four—times a day, and they usually involve asking for strength against temptation...at least where Steffan Carmichael is concerned.

At least Ava has been on cloud nine. She and Bryce have been texting since having pizza on the terrace. He even came to the room once. Nothing serious—yet—has happened, but I'm so excited for her. He seems like a genuinely nice guy. Who is apparently lucky to be alive. Ava told me Bryce has a prosthetic leg. That's why his name was so familiar. I thought he was the one who got his leg ripped off by an alligator! To my embarrassment, Ava told him about me thinking he was the alligator attack victim. But Bryce laughed, saying that was some crazy rumor that got started. He was in a horrific hunting accident that resulted in his leg being amputated below the knee. He being an athlete, combined with his young age, helped him make a quick recovery. She's planning to attend some physical therapy sessions with him, so I guess you could say there's definitely something happening between these two. It's exciting for me because I feel like I've been there from their first meeting, and while I'm not trying to sound creepy, I'm totally invested and kind of a part of this. I'm actually on my way to our room right now to ask Ava if she wants to invite Bryce to the movies with me and Kali.

I've grown a lot closer to Kali over the past few weeks. She and I have gone for coffee every Monday and Wednesday after class. That's my new routine. Go to class, hate but secretly crush over Steffan, and then go complain about him to Kali over coffee. After that, I go rehash everything with Ava.

I unlock my dorm door and call out as I push it open, "You'll never—"

My backpack falls to the floor as a scream rips from my throat. It's not registering what is in front of me. I can't process what my eyes are seeing. Ava's lying on the floor, her body at an odd angle. There's red liquid on the floor that is so dark, it's almost black. The green bedsheets hang off the sides, and have damp spots on them and there's what appears to be puddles next to the body. Ava's body. At least I think it's her, but maybe it's not.

That's not Ava. That can't be Ava. The skin color is wrong. That's not Ava. But my mind tells me that it is, that she's the only one who would be in our room.

I try to yell for help but only a squeak comes out. I open my mouth again and push for a sound, but only air hisses through. My knees crack as they hit the floor. I feel dizzy. The room is spinning, and there's a funny smell in the air. All the red stained sheets are swirling together.

My eyes come into focus slightly when I see movement. *Is she still alive?* Hope blooms in my chest. I crawl over toward her, but stop when my fingers come into contact with the pool of blood on the floor. I stand and wait for movement again.

"Ava?" My voice is hoarse, almost as though I've been screaming, yet I haven't managed to make another sound since I first opened the door.

There's movement, but it's in Ava's hair. Her hair is moving. My body is violently trembling, but I have to get closer. On shaky legs, I stand and step around the puddle of blood. I ignore the tiny drops and blood spatter on the walls and dripping from the ceiling.

Bile rises in my throat as I see the vacant look in her eyes and her slack jaw. There's an angry slash along her slender throat and on both wrists. Tears fall down my face, but I still can't seem to form words or even a sound. Silent sobs shake my body as I see my lifeless friend. I lean over to examine her thick brown hair that's splayed out over the floor. I could've sworn I saw something move.

My hand hovers over her hair, my fingertips about to graze the strands, when I hear a hiss and two fangs appear. I jump back as the snake shoots forward at me. Its black beady eyes staring at me with its mouth open. Another one appears then, and its forked tongue seems to almost wave at me.

Oh my God. Snakes? Snakes...

My mind instantly goes back to last year and a voice saying... *"I'm a snake, Little Mouse."*

CHAPTER FIVE

Steffan

The red and blue lights swirling around campus are hard to ignore. So is the image of a black body bag being carried out of the girls' dorms that has been circulating over the past few days on social media. Everyone is being questioned, and right now, anyone with access to the dorms is a suspect. Having the police so active on campus is really making things difficult for me and the guys to get our business done. I understood a chick died and all, but shipments are still coming in and I need to make sure they are not being stopped on their way back off campus. I feel on edge and slightly irritated. Even hanging out in the quad between classes hasn't been as relaxing for me as it used to be.

"They're ruling it a *murder*. No evidence of a suicide because the angle of the cuts couldn't have been self-inflected, or something," Summer gossips in my ear. "I heard that the room was covered in so much blood that they had to close it down for the whole semester," she continues, and I feel the urge to correct her. I'm not in the mood to hear about a murder that was probably some fit of rage or jealousy between girls.

"Well, I hope they catch whoever did it soon," Lee comments, and I can hear the low tone of irritation in his voice, the same one that mimics my own.

Ever since the murder, Summer has glued herself to my side. She's always been overly affectionate, but lately, she's been downright clingy. I already have enough on my plate, so trying to dodge her in order to get business done, as well, is only adding to my stress. Her continuous presence also means less time for Lee and me to plan and move forward with the next set of initiation games for the pledges.

"I just can't believe they found a snake!" Summer's friend shudders dramatically.

My gaze slides to Stella...or maybe her name is Celeste. "What snake?"

"You didn't hear?" Her eyes widen when I shake my head no. "Oh my God, it was the strangest thing, but when they moved the body, snakes were tangled in her hair. They had to call animal control."

Summer nods. "Yeah and the snakes were venomous."

My brow rises, but I don't comment. It's been days, and the story around campus has changed every time I hear it. At this point, I doubt anyone besides the girl's roommate actually knows what happened.

"I'm heading to class." I nod to Lee, before pushing off the bench. Across the quad, my gaze lands on the person I did want to see: one of our newest brothers.

"Hey, Brandon!" I shout and watch with mild fascination at how fast the guy turns around, his face paling a little from the sound of my voice.

"Uh, hey." His voice shakes, but he manages to at least look me in the eyes.

"You still have that connection in the admissions office?"

He looks around, like he's trying to make sure no one heard me, before lowering his voice. "Sort of. Jerry, my roommate, he works in the office. I can get in after hours if I take his key."

"Yeah, right. You mean Jerry, your boyfriend?" I confirm, shrugging my shoulders. I want him to know I'm aware of their real relationship, and I'm trusting them both with the information I'm giving. Not that anybody would give a shit.

Brandon's face flushes. "Ah, yeah. What do you need?"

I dip my hand into my pocket and take out some cash before handing it to him. "Here, this is for you. I need to know everything about this girl," I tell him, before handing him a piece of paper sitting on top of the wad of money.

"Taylor Mae Lake," he mumbles quietly. "I'll get it to you."

I nod and brush past him as I walk away. Another task done. I can't explain why, but I feel like I need to know more about my little psych partner. Not only does my grade in class depend on our ability to work together, but I have the feeling she knows something about what happened last year at the Halloween party. As much as I enjoy our sparring in class, I can't get it out of my head that she holds some animosity toward me and I think it somehow all started that night. I need to eliminate any possible threats, too, no matter how small or insignificant they may seem.

Jose Suco catches up to me and walks in step with me back toward where I left Lee. Jose clears his throat and speaks. "Brother Carmichael. At football practice, this guy showed up today. He used to be on the team, but his name sounded familiar."

I don't have time for this shit. I stop walking and stare him down. "Get to the point."

To his credit, he doesn't back down. "Bryce Van Doren."

"Repeat that."

"Bryce Van Doren."

Impossible. We banished him. Fucker almost died. There's no way he would dare show his face back here. He's the reason my twin isn't running Delta Pi Theta with me. A part of me wishes he had died, but that would have only raised more issues.

"You must've been mistaken. Are you sure he said his name was Van Doren?"

"Yes, sir. Redhead. In shape. Prosthetic leg."

"Fuck." What's Van Doren doing back at Thorn University? He recovered faster than I expected. And he has more balls than I gave him credit for by showing back up here. We'll have to find him and remind him of his current standing with us. Shouldn't be too hard to do since he's walking around like he hasn't a care in the world. *Son of a bitch.*

"Back the fuck up!" I turn around right as some guy wearing a football jersey steps up to Lee, ready to fight. The small group we had been sitting with flanks Lee's sides, but the guy also has friends with him. My eyes flick down to Lee's hands and watch as he shoves them into the pocket of his jeans. Having known Lee almost all my life, I know he's about to attack.

"We have a problem?" I whistle to gain the football player's attention. The minute his head snaps in my direction, I recognize him. Kasper Kyle. Thorn University's prized wide receiver, and ex-best friend of Bryce Van Doren.

Kasper is the first to look away. "No problem," he manages to squeeze out, a deep, angry flush creeping up his neck.

"Let's keep it that way, shall we?" Lee responds, stepping around Kasper and his friends, each of them held in place by fear.

With one last glance, Lee and I make our way across the quad to class. At this rate, I'm going to be late, not that I care, but I hate having to pretend that I'm sorry for it.

"What was his problem?" I ask Lee, lowering my voice.

Lee shakes his head. "No idea. He was spouting off. Something about his girl being all over me at the party last weekend."

I cock my brow. "He was ready to fight you here in the quad over that?"

"You clearly haven't seen his girlfriend."

"Idiot."

"Maybe. He might make good gator bait, though."

"Shut the fuck up." I laugh.

Lee looks around, and I instantly feel the hairs on my neck rise. "There's a rumor going around that Van Doren is back on campus."

Speaking of gator bait. "So I hear."

"He's connected to the campus murder."

"Excuse me?" I lean closer, not sure I heard him right.

Lee nods, his eyes darting around once more, ensuring that the crowd behind us has dispersed. "Rumor is someone saw him talking to the chick who just ended up dead."

"He knows he can't be here," I respond through gritted teeth, my anger simmering just below the surface, while I keep my outside appearance calm and collected. "He'll be a dead man if he so much as shows his face in front of us."

"We both know the Van Dorens will push the matter to the end. There's also a chance he's here to look for...you know," Lee trails off.

Soren.

If Bryce feels that he's owed something because of what happened that night, he'd definitely be after Soren.

I need to send out a mass text to the brothers to be on the lookout. Before I can even open my texts, though, my phone vibrates with an incoming message from my father.

Dad: He's gone.

"Fuck," I mutter under my breath. So much for class today.

My eyes start to burn hours later, and I finally make it to my room and collapse on the bed. My head spins from all the information we gathered through the evening and into the early morning. After a brief conversation with my dad, it was confirmed that Soren left his boarding school overseas. There was one hit on his passport, returning to the United States a week ago, but no one has seen him since. I'm pissed at my father for just now telling me. He's been missing for days! He didn't go home. He hasn't set foot in Blue Rose, Alabama. He's become a ghost. Lee and I scoured security footage from bus stops, and we were just about to start on car rental stations when I needed a break. My head throbs, and my chest feels tight. I miss Soren, but I'm not sure it's safe for him to be here. Too many questions came out of the incident last Halloween. Too much attention was brought to the fraternity, and subsequently, to The Illicit. While some members stood by my father's choice, there were others who felt he was too close to crossing the very thin line on whether or not Bryce had deserved his almost death. Many thought Soren should have had to answer for his role in the fight, but before it could happen, he had been shipped off. I was the deciding factor in his fate, agreeing with my father that Soren should escape overseas until things calm down.

Now he's returned.

But why?

I don't know how long I've been lying here when I hear a sharp knock on my door, followed by a bang, which has me sitting up. "What?"

"Steff, you need to get out here!" Lee's voice carries through the door. I jump up from the urgency in his tone and throw on a pair of sweats before the door is thrown open.

"The hell—"

"You need to get out here now," Lee rushes out, pushing me into the hallway, where different brothers are lurking and waiting. A few of them look pale, almost sickly.

"What happened?"

Lee shakes his head. By the time my feet hit the stairs, more of the guys are rushing into the front entryway. My heart hammers in my chest. I can sense that something dark is waiting for me on the other side of the door. There's a copper smell in the air, and judging by the look on everyone's faces, it's bad. I can feel the touch of death before my hand even reaches for the door handle and shivers run down my arms. Jose appears on my left, his head lowers. Whatever I'm about to see, is already setting me on edge. I can feel my stomach sinking as if a lead brick was dropped on it. It physically hurts to move, to breathe.

Soren.

I throw the door open, unprepared for the amount of blood spatter and gore that greets me. Strung between the two white columns that frame our front door is Kasper Kyle's massacred body. "Fuck."

"What do we do?" Lee asks, and I glance at him. His fist is in front of his mouth like he's trying to block the coppery smell of blood and the sour tang from the ripped and mutilated flesh that is heavy in the air.

My eyes trail over Kasper, or what's left of him. His arms and legs are spread-eagle between the columns, tied with the intestines that are clearly missing from his torso cavity. His mouth and eyes are open in terror, the muscles tight from the rigor mortis already setting in.

"Wait!" Jose rushes to the side and grabs a stick off the bush. "Did you see that?"

"His lack of organs?" I ask, my voice laced in sarcasm.

"His throat." Jose moves closer. "It moved."

I step forward, eyes focused on the purple handprints decorating his neck. Then I see it, the column of his throat ripples. "Something is in there."

I pull my knife from my pocket and move toward the body.

"The cops are already on the way," Lee warns. "Don't give them a reason to find your prints on anything."

Jose moves closer again, his face pulled tight, before shoving the end of the stick into Kasper's gaping mouth. "I got it." When he pulls back, a long, black snake is coiled around the stick. "Shit!"

He drops the stick, but everyone's eyes move back to Kasper's throat, as it bobs and pulls in different directions. "There's more in there."

"This is so fucked up," Lee murmurs, his eyes glued to the snake currently recoiling itself on the ground.

Sirens soon sound in the distance, which means we only have so much time before our house becomes a crime scene, and the men in blue are swarming our space. "Get the house in order," I throw over my shoulder. "Take pictures," I instruct Lee, who pulls his phone out and snaps multiple pictures. "Also, question all the brothers. I want to know where everyone was and who they were with. Make sure nobody speaks to the police without an attorney. Get one of our officers on the inside to be present during questioning. Set up a meeting to find out what they all know."

"Jose." I turn to him. "Get Nathaniel. You two check the security cameras. Go through all the footage. Twice." I keep my gaze focused on the blue and red lights getting closer and closer from the long road that leads to our house. Being the most secluded Greek house has its advantages, it's off on its own, surrounded by trees with a long-ass drive, perfect for hiding the shady shit we do. *And now a murder has been committed in broad daylight.* Everybody has been in and out of the house. How did no one hear this fucker scream?

"Louie!" I bark out. He runs up to me. "Gather all the pledges. Every single one. Find out who was on the grounds today. Who spoke to Kasper, who has class with him, or anyone on the football team, find me anyone who even just crossed paths with him in the past twenty-four hours. Somebody *has* to have heard or saw something. Drill these fuckers about everything they did today, from what they ate to when they shit."

Someone is messing with the brotherhood by bringing this attention to our door.

More importantly...Soren is still missing.

My phone rings, and I see it's Brandon.

"Whatcha got for me?"

"Taylor Mae Lake. She's from bumfuck nowhere Mississippi. Super religious little community with a squeaky-clean upbringing. Very involved in her church that is led by Brother and Sister Myers. Her roommate was the girl who was murdered. She's in a new room in the West building. This girl is basically a nobody with a spotless, boring-ass history. All she does is work at the library, study for her classes, complete volunteer work, and love Jesus."

"Friends?"

"Her only friend is dead. That's the only red flag that's popped up. Other than you showing interest."

No friends. No party life. Then our paths couldn't have crossed, so why does she automatically hate me? And why do I care?

I end the call without another word. I'm wound up and can't think clearly. I don't have time for some holy roller, wide-eyed country bumpkin getting under my skin. Then I remember her watching me...

A small smile forms as I text Summer and tell her to meet me at our usual spot in the library. Sirens wail. People are still scrambling around. Fuck them. Kasper was a dick, so I don't care about his death, but I am pissed it's brought this shitshow to our doorstep.

I turn to Lee. "Have Jose answer their questions. If they want to speak to me, have them set up an interview. Right now, there is no evidence that points to one of us as the murderer.

There are too many of us, which means they can't arrest anyone in particular."

His eyes widen slightly. "You're leaving?'

I tilt my head and shrug. "You should too. Anyone passing through the quad the other day will know Kasper had an issue with you. If they find you here, conveniently at the scene..." I let my voice trail off. "Go figure out an alibi."

I glance back at Jose. "No one gets taken into custody. We will comply with interviews, if asked or if there is a warrant." Jose nods at me, before shifting his gaze back to Kasper's body.

I manage to slip back into the house and grab some clothes before taking off into the trees and disappearing. When I get back, I'll handle everything as I usually do. Make some calls, discuss what happened with my father so he can make The Illicit aware, and then Lee and I will sit down and interrogate every single pledge and Scab with access to the house until their stories are airtight. Hopefully by the time I get back, our tech guy will also have video footage for us to see. Until then, I need a release and the idea of riling Taylor fucking Mae up brings me the first smile I've had all damn day.

When I first walk into the library, I don't see her. Anger boils within me that I made this trip for nothing. Then I see the back of someone who looks like an extra for *Little House on the Prairie.* Her shiny hair is in a side braid. That vision makes me want to wrap my fingers around it and drag her to the back of the library. Demand she tell me why her eyes always follow me, and ask her if she knows why I like it. Force her to meet my eyes as I hike her dress up and find out if this is a one-sided attraction. Then laugh if she's wet and leave her that way for fucking with my head.

As if she senses me, she turns around. Those doe eyes meet mine, and I smirk, causing her to frown. I never take my eyes off her as I walk past her on my way toward my usual spot. *Come on, little one. I know you want to watch.*

I lean against the wall of books and close my eyes. *Soren. My father. Van Doren. Kasper.* So many fucking problems. Plus, we have shipments to deliver. New pledges to train. Bullshit fronts to keep up. I hear the shuffle of feet and feel a faint smile. *But all those problems can wait for a few minutes.*

I open my eyes to see a cute little braid between the cracks, moving on the other side of the shelf. Trying to be sneaky, trying to blend into the library books and failing miserably, because she knows I see her.

"I hope you haven't been waiting for long, babe." Summer's high-pitched voice comes from my right, but I don't spare her a glance. I simply gesture for her to come to me, using two fingers. When Summer is within reach, I grab her by the hips and pull her to me.

A set of brown eyes finally meet mine. *There you are...*

My eyes burn into Taylor's as I slide my hands under Summer's clothes and roam them all over her body. I spin Summer around so her front is facing Taylor. I hear the tiny gasps from both of them. Summer's head falls back on me, but I don't even fucking blink, as I challenge Taylor with my eyes to look away. I slide my hand down the front of Summer's shorts. In clear view of Taylor's watchful eyes. But it's not enough.

I roughly jerk Summer's shorts and panties down. Taylor's eyebrows rise as her eyes zero in on my fingers, spreading Summer's soaked lips as I ravage her cunt. Her eyes come back to mine, and I cock a brow, an unspoken question in my stare

Do you want this to be you?

Taylor gasps and steps back from the shelves. Her head turns away, not wanting to watch, but I know she's just as turned on as I am, so I insert two fingers with enough force to get a moan out of Summer. *That* gets her attention. Taylor's eyes make their way back to the show.

I'll give you something to watch, little church mouse.

Summer orgasms around my fingers. I pull them out and stick them between her lips, which she greedily takes.

"I've got some things to take care of," I whisper to Summer with my eyes still on Taylor.

"Don't you need—"

"No."

"Suit yourself. Thanks, babe." And she walks away from me.

My eyes remain on Taylor, whose eyes are staring at the bulge in my pants. She probably thinks it's from Summer. Hardly. Summer has barely left the aisle, and I'm already unbuckling my pants. I quickly free then fist my erection. To really fuck with her, I push myself off the wall. I prop one arm against the shelf she's on the other side of and lean down until I'm at eye level with her. I roughly jerk myself off, all the while staring into her dark, brown eyes, moaning while I envision that it's Taylor's hands wrapped around my cock.

I bet I could reach through and grab her hand right now and she'd finish the job. I can't see it, but I bet she's squeezing her legs together.

"Not so innocent, little Taylor Mae. What would Brother and Sister Myers think?"

There's a tiny squeak, and then I hear the sound of her feet hurrying away, just as I finish myself off to the memory of her watchful eyes.

CHAPTER SIX

Taylor

How'd he find out? I've been freaking out all afternoon, and now I'm struggling to fall asleep. How does Steffan know who Brother and Sister Myers are? Does that mean he knows *him?* He'd have to, if he knows *them.* They're my minister and his wife, and *his* adoptive parents. I close my eyes and I see *his* face. Telling me how precious I am. Reminding me that I'm his. "*You were created for me. This was all preordained,*" he reminds me. The Lord created me for *him,* his voice repeats in my ear like a chant only he believes. *His hands shake as they hover up my thigh.* I squeeze my eyes shut and force myself to go to sleep, knowing I'll regret it. Once he's in my head, the nightmares will follow.

"*Remember, only a whore spreads her legs. We have to fight these sinful urges. You're so precious, Taylor. Promise you'll remain pure for me. Keep clean what's mine. The Lord created such a beautiful woman for me, but the Devil tempts me.*" The gleam of a blade startles me. "*Shush now. Don't be alarmed. I have to fight the demons. I know what to do.*" I shriek as I feel the warm drops of his blood on my knee as he presses the blade into his palm. "*Now...*" He groans. "*Now I shall not be tempted further."* He slaps his injured hand on my exposed knee, and I cringe as I feel the sticky wetness against my skin. *"It would help if you'd wear longer skirts,"* he fumes through gritted teeth as he painfully squeezes my knee. *Tears build in my eyes, but he continues to squeeze harder. We both cry out when he finally releases me. His other hand holds his injured one as he gasps from the pain.*

The vision changes...and now I see snakes. Ava lying on the floor with her hair fanned out around her. Her hair is moving as though it's floating on water, but the fluid motions are coming from the slithering of snakes. They rise up, coil back, and then strike at me. Their fangs dig into my skin, sending immense pain. They wrap around my arms and neck, tightening with unbelievable strength. I look down, and there's blood everywhere. A deep voice echoes in a whisper somewhere in the distance that resembles more of a hissing sound, *"Little Mousssse."*

A scream rips through my throat and then there's a loud banging.

"Taylor! *Taylor!* Open the door! Taylor! Let us in!"

With a violent jerk, my body finally wakes up. The banging continues, though, and I realize that someone is actually knocking on my door. I throw off my covers and then slide out of bed. "Coming!" I call out as I rush toward my *new* dorm door, since my other room is now a crime scene.

I pull open the door to find my floor's resident advisor and two other girls standing outside in the hallway, still wearing their pajamas.

"Taylor," my RA, Latoya, studies me with concerned eyes, "are you okay? We heard you scream."

Heat creeps up my neck into my cheeks. I avert her gaze by studying my bare feet. "I had a nightmare." I leave the "again" unspoken. This is becoming a problem. It's the third night in a row I've woken up the entire floor by screaming.

"You're drenched in sweat." She sighs, and then I feel her arms wrap around me. "I'm sure you'll have those for a while. You need to talk to someone."

"I am. I'm going to the counselor this week." It's a lie. They scheduled an appointment for me, but I'm not planning to attend.

"I'm sorry. Want one of us to bunk with you for the night? Or you can come to one of our rooms." I pull back and then shake my head. She gives me a skeptical look, and then her shoulders drop with another exhausted sigh. "Hopefully we can find you a roommate tomorrow."

Ugh. I hate the idea of having to start all over with a stranger. Plus, I feel like I'm replacing Ava. It's silly to think that, but she was the best roommate. And...she was my friend.

"I'm sorry. I'm okay now, you all should go back to bed." Mortification has me turning red as I meet each of their tired eyes.

Latoya leans closer to me and says, "We understand. I'm surprised you're still finishing the semester."

I was given the option to take the semester off, since my roommate was murdered, and I was the one to find her. But what am I going to do? I like getting lost in my studies and books, so I might as well stay here. I can have nightmares here, just as well as I can at home, only there I'll be behind a semester and within *his* reach. My parents completely panicked when I called them. They demanded I return home immediately. But I can't go back to *him*. At one time, I loved the idea of being his. He was the first boy to notice me. My first boyfriend, if you could call him that. Everything was perfect, almost like a small-town romance novel...that is, until he turned obsessive, controlling, and downright frightening. Was it all his raging hormones? Was it really me tempting him all the time that made him that way? If I had stayed, would things have turned out differently if I gave him what he wanted? No. He was psycho. He treated me like a possession. I made the right decision in getting as far away as possible. Ava's death might forever haunt me, but I won't run from this terror like I did from him. I'll face every demon that's out there before I go back.

The question is, who did this? Who killed Ava, and why? Who's lurking the hallways? There's a gnawing in my gut. My worst fear is I brought this upon Ava somehow. Could *he* have followed me? But I don't know how. I don't know anything anymore.

I tell Latoya and everyone goodnight and close my door. Now I'm wide awake and still have three hours before class. *Great.* I swipe my phone screen and hope to spend some time mindlessly scrolling through social media. To not think about the police interviews and all their questions. Their tone laced with suspicion that I could be Ava's killer. No amount of funny memes or cat videos will push away the sight of Ava's lifeless body from my mind.

My chat pings.

Kali: What are you doing awake?

Me: Couldn't sleep. You?

Kali: Finishing a project. Are you okay?

Me: Yes. No. I don't know.

Kali: On my way.

What? She's coming across campus at this hour? Five minutes later and there's another knock at my door. I unlock the door and allow Kali inside. She has her backpack and a cute dress on a hanger. She holds it up and shrugs. "I have a presentation in four hours. Figured I'd crash here for a cat nap."

"You came all the way over here to sleep?" I ask in disbelief.

"You're still having trouble sleeping after what happened. And rightfully so. That was...gruesome. Maybe having a friend here will help you."

Gruesome doesn't even begin to cover it. Psychotic is more like it. Horrific. I mean, there were *snakes,* and the police said the blood was intentionally drained from her body.

"Did you...did you hear what happened at the Delta Pi Theta house?"

I feel all the color drain from my face. The Delta Pi Theta house is where Steffan lives. My life changed forever inside that house. I shake my head. Kali shifts her weight from side to side and refuses to meet my eyes. "What happened?"

"There's been another murder. A guy this time. This murder also involved snakes, just like your roommate. You know that a snake is on their fraternity's crest, right? It's a snake wrapped around a dagger."

"They found snakes in his hair?" I swallow the lump in my throat and fight the nauseous feeling in my stomach.

"Worse. In his throat. It was our university's star football player. He was found on Delta Pi Theta's porch, body stretched between the two big columns, guts hanging out...freaking gutted like an animal. Rumor is he'd been arguing with Lee Concord." Kali rolls her eyes. "Stupid. He should've known better than to talk shit to one of the brothers."

My eyes blink rapidly as I try to process the words coming out of Kali's mouth. "Because he is in a frat?"

Her eyebrows rise. "Not just any frat. Delta Pi Theta pretty much runs this campus. Their fraternity has the best parties too. Everyone wants an 'in' with them. They're all mysterious and closed off. Ugh, and Lee Concord definitely gives off big dick energy. Lucky you that your class project partner is part of it, too."

I scoff. "I know nothing about him and don't care to." *That's a little bit of a lie.* "I barely tolerate him, and I'm sure the feeling is mutual." I shut up and wait for her to tell me what she knows. I want to tell Kali that Steffan somehow found out stuff about me that I didn't tell him, but I'm afraid that conversation will lead to another one about what happened in the library when I watched him with that blonde, again, but this time, he watched *me* back. He went as far as acknowledging my presence.

She's quiet for a moment and then sighs. "You didn't hear it from me, but the story is they're more than a college frat. Mafia-gang-type shit. And it's not a stretch to believe these murders are their doing. Especially with how secretive they are. They never let anyone too close. I even heard rumors that they have underground fight nights and that's how they afford their house. Pledges who don't make it in their frat drop out then disappear. Haven't you heard any of this?"

My heart is beating so hard in my chest. He told me he was a snake. Kali said the football player should've known better than to argue with one of the fraternity brothers...but—no. Steffan wouldn't have killed my roommate because I got an attitude with him. That's ridiculous. If anything, it would've been the new boyfriend, right? But she wasn't really dating Bryce. I'm accusing this nice guy over someone who came out and told me he was a snake and could possibly be in a gang and they're just going around killing people on campus. I'm letting my crush cloud my judgment. Yet, there's no motive for Ava's murder.

A chilling thought crosses my mind. Did he finally remember who I am? Is he angry I didn't say anything or remind him? I hope he didn't remember. I hope I remain forgotten. That he never recalls having slept with me.

Is that it? Not thanking him for sleeping with me and then ditching me? Would he have taken that as a snub? I went back, but he'd left. Something tells me that tidbit of information wouldn't matter to him. I'm so confused. So many damn questions. Why would he hurt Ava? I'm the only connecting link.

"Taylor? Are you okay? Did something happen?"

"No," I reply a little too quickly. "I'm a little shook up over another murder happening, and so soon. Steffan wasn't in class today either...so it's creeping me out." *But he was in the library.* Lord help me, why did I stand there and watch him like that? What's wrong with me? Has coming here turned me into a whore? Have I let the sins of the flesh corrupt my mind? Then again, a part of me wonders that if I become so tainted, will all my fears vanish? I'll no longer be pure, sweet, innocent Taylor Mae. I'd be free. However, I don't want to sacrifice my soul's salvation, either. My mind is all over the place. I just feel that these days I'm walking a fine line.

"Hey," Kali speaks softly, and I meet her eyes, "I'm here."

"Thanks. I do feel better having you here. There has been a lot going on." I pause. "Hey, Kali?"

"Yeah?"

"If it's so secretive, I mean, I've never heard of it, but then how do you know so much about it?"

She smiles. "Let's just say I might have a history with one of the guys." Then her face turns serious. "But mum's the word. They go insane about keeping their secrets. He would literally kill me and you for knowing. Any of them would."

All the blood drains from my face. Kali giggles. "Stop. You look like you're going to be sick. Besides, it's probably not even true. Just because everyone who rushes that frat go on to become the most successful men in the world doesn't mean the rumors about them being part of the mafia are real. It's probably just a coincidence. Anyway, let's change the subject. You know, I hate my roommate. And this dorm is so much nicer. Would you want to be roomies?"

"Are you sure you want to move into this dorm? With the girl whose roommate was killed?"

"Possibly."

I laugh, and it feels strange to be laughing after everything we've discussed, but I can't help it. Kali joins in, which only causes me to laugh harder. Tears stream down my face and I fall over on my side on the bed. "That works for me. My RA is looking for a new roommate for me, and it would be nice to have someone I already somewhat know."

Kali scoffs. "Don't get too excited over the idea."

We both laugh again, and then I say, "I'm sorry. I really am excited."

She smiles and tilts her head. "Me too. I believe this is the start of an exciting escapade!"

Wednesday comes and I know I'm going to have to face Steffan at some point. He wasn't in class on Monday and I doubt he'd skip twice in one week. I couldn't be that lucky. I'm a nervous wreck as I walk to my psychology class. I also have the eerie feeling I'm being watched, which is making me paranoid. I keep looking over my shoulder as I walk past the campus landscape of trees, bushes, and all the other things a killer could be hiding behind. Shuddering, I pick up my pace, both eager and anxious to get to class. At least Kali, who has turned out to be a fantastic roommate and friend, will also be there, with my coffee that she left earlier than me to go get. I swear she's a bigger caffeine addict that I am.

After what she told me, I have to find a way to prove Steffan is the murderer. A mafia frat? What the hell? Of course, he did it! Ava deserves to have her murderer stand trial. Him saying he's a snake, then the killer leaves FREAKING LIVE SNAKES by Ava's body and inside the football player's body, like some serial killer calling card. It's creepy and way too coincidental. Plus, the fact that he hasn't been around lately only makes me more suspicious, like he's out covering his tracks. It all connects, but I need proof. I can't just go to the police and say these things. They'll need evidence or a motive. There's also the question of how to go about this and not end up the victim of a crazed killer.

My God. I'm also his partner on this project. As much as I hate the idea, that's going to be my ticket to get close to him. I'll need to be smart and cautious about this. My stomach tightens just thinking about trying to talk to him, let alone confront him. I walk into class and Kali is already there. She hands me my coffee and I give her a small smile as I take my seat. I force myself to stop trembling because he can't hurt me while I'm here. And at least I arrived before him. So I wait, my heart beating a hundred miles an hour. And I wait some more. Until the professor starts with today's lecture.

An hour and a half later, all my nerves were for nothing. Steffan never showed.

I leave the classroom furious. There goes my plan to kick-start solving Ava's murder, because I obviously can't talk to him if he isn't here. Plus, we're supposed to be partners, and we have a project that's due in two weeks. Kali catches up to me as I'm practically stomping down the hall with my books clutched to my chest.

"Hey, what's going on?"

I stop in the middle of the hallway to turn and face Kali. "He didn't show up. Again!"

"I thought you were scared of him."

"I am! Obviously. I mean, duh, he's clearly a psychopath."

Kali looks around at the people walking past us. "Lower your voice. You don't want word getting back that you're bad-mouthing them." She leans forward and whispers, "Isn't it a good thing that you didn't have to sit next to him...and talk to him? I'm not following why you're so upset."

"Because we still have a project due that's fifty percent of my grade. I could lose my scholarship. My future could be ruined."

I can't stop the tears from coming. I despise the fact that I'm crying here in the middle of a crowded hallway, but it's like all of the trauma and the emotion that I've dealt with the past few days has finally bubbled to the surface. I'm so damn scared and frustrated. I wasn't there when Ava died in our room, and I need to get justice for her by helping to find out who killed her. Then that person can be removed from campus and locked away in prison for the rest of his life. Maybe then I will get closure—and some sleep would be nice. My entire life is riding on how I perform academically, as well. There's a lot of pressure on me right now and Steffan seems to be at the center of it.

"Whoa! It's okay, it's okay."

I angrily wipe away tears with my hand. "I cry when I'm mad, okay? And right now...I'm *furious*." With a growl, I turn and stomp out of the building.

I need to be alone and rage by myself. Everything is so messed up. I have to figure out my life. I need some way to salvage this project. I can't allow a drop in my GPA to cause me to lose my scholarship and unravel my well-laid plans for a successful future. A future out from under my parents' thumb, and a guaranteed ticket away from *him*. This project is also my only chance to talk to Steffan and figure out how I can connect him to Ava's murder.

Tears continue to fall, which only pisses me off even more. Horrible and foul words that I can call Steffan cross my mind. My emotions are so high that I might be tempted to use that kind of language, if I saw him right now.

"Taylor?"

I spin around in the direction of the male voice. "Bryce?"

I haven't seen the handsome and charming redhead since the night before Ava... I don't even want to finish that thought. He offers me a sad smile. He must be thinking the same thing.

"Hi." He gives me a weak wave. Then his eyes narrow and he takes a step closer. His voice is gentle as he asks, "Are you okay?"

"Y-yeah. Why?" I say this so casually, like I don't have tears streaming down my face.

"Your," he points to my cheek and then his own, "it's running. There's black stuff, goopy lines down your face."

"Oh my gosh!" I fumble to balance my books while I shrug off my backpack. *Why didn't I put my books in my bag when I left class?* Oh, that's right! Because I decided to leave class in a temper tantrum, and now I'm crying stupid, angry tears and walking around campus looking like a bad circus clown.

Bryce takes my books and holds them for me. I offer him a grateful smile and then quickly unzip my backpack. I always pack baby wipes, because you never know when you might spill something or have to touch a gross door handle. The only other time I've been this grateful that I have this habit was when I was in the bathroom stall at the student center and there was no toilet paper. Turning my back to Bryce, I wipe under my eyes and down my cheeks. I blow my nose and then take a deep, long breath. I exhale and then face him, ready to take my books. As I'm placing my books in my bags, he shoves his hands into the pockets of his fitted khakis. I can easily see why Ava was so crazy about him. He's handsome, muscular, and has kind blue eyes. Not the piercing and intense blue eyes like a certain psychopath I know.

"I'm sorry I haven't come to check on you. I know we were only just getting to know each other, but I really liked Ava. I hope we can keep in touch. Or would it be weird?" He visibly cringes and then he holds a hand up. "I'm sorry." He backs up and starts to turn away.

"Wait," I call out to him. When he turns around, I ask, "Why would it be weird?"

"I don't know. Seeing you so upset makes me feel like a real dick that I've not reached out sooner. I was afraid to; the police thought I was a suspect. Can you believe that?"

When I don't answer, he pales. "Or do you believe it?"

"No. I don't believe that. Of course not." The police did ask me questions about Bryce, but I already know who did it. I just need to figure out how to prove it and get justice for Ava.

"Good. I was really worried you'd think that and be scared of me. The seed would be planted and all that, ya know?"

"Because you guys were talking and hanging out? That doesn't make you capable of something so vile."

"Listen, I'd really like to catch up. I've got to get to class, but how about we go out for a pizza tonight?" He gives me a crooked smile. "With pineapples?"

I bite back a smile but can't stop the blush heating my cheeks. He remembered. Guilt washes over me. Of course, he did. That's when he met my recently-murdered roommate, who he was about to start dating. I am the worst friend, roommate, and person walking this planet. "I work tonight, actually. It'll be late when I'm finished."

"All the more reason for me to escort you back to the dorms. I'll get the pizza, and then pick you up. At least let me do that. Please? I'd feel a lot better if I made sure you made it to your dorm safely."

I want to remind him that Ava was in the dorm, where she was supposedly safe, but instead, I agree for him to pick me up from the library at nine.

I hate myself. Despite my own personal self-loathing and feelings of guilt, I'm in a cheery mood at the thought of Bryce arriving in an hour. Frustration eats at me for being excited; yet, I can't *stop* grinning because I have these butterflies. I don't have much experience with dating, and what little I have done is nothing to smile about. Now here's this cute and sweet guy coming to see me. Only problem is, he's my dead roommate's last love interest. Clearly my type is emotionally damaged, which is a total red flag. But that's not his fault, so technically, it shouldn't count against him. Then again, if I'm arguing with myself over having pizza with this guy, that in and of itself should be a warning sign. It's not like it's a date, though, I guess it just feels weird. I'll ask Kali if this makes me a terrible friend.

The library is completely empty other than me and Lois. Sweet, sweet Lois. She's well over sixty, the size of a toothpick, with thinning, red-orange hair that she teases up to look like a constant glowing fireball, and her coffee-stained teeth always have her maroon lipstick on them. I absolutely adore her. She's full of spunk, and, because I'm certain she suffers from a little bit of dementia, every day is a new day. For instance, every other day, I get to hear the story of her with Walter Dupree in the cornfield and the two of them stealing a police car. The first time I heard it, I almost went into a panic attack, because I knew someone who shared the same last name. But then it felt silly. To let one person ruin a name for everyone who shares it. It's like when people won't name their kid something because they knew someone in elementary school with that name. It goes back to allowing a single individual to hold so much power because of a few letters of the alphabet. I've learned not to let it bother me; in fact, I'm envious that Lois had such an incredible and romantic night that, after all these years, she's still holding on to it.

Her head slightly bobbles as she trots toward me. "Did you read the title of some of these romance novels?" She holds up a clearly erotic one. My cheeks heat, because, of course, I've seen it, and I might have devoured it in a few quick reads on my breaks. "Takes me back to my younger days. When I was your age, there's no way I'd be stuck in here. Not when boys look like they do now. Lawd have mercy. What are they feeding 'em? They're putting some kind of enhancement in the food, have to be." She places the book on the shelf. "They sure are built differently. A whole new breed of stallions. But do they know what to do with those powerful bodies? All that muscle. Long limbs— well, we can only hope for a certain limb to be long. But not just the length is important. Gotta have some girth." Her thin brows furrow and she holds up a long, bony finger. "The main thing is they know how to use the tools that the good Lord gave 'em. Otherwise, looks won't get 'em very far."

Well, that's one way to put it. After all, we were taught in church to use the talents God instilled in us. A slow smile spreads across her face. Although this coming from Lois is funny, I pray that she'll stop talking before this conversation goes any further down a very dirty and uncomfortable path. But I see that wistful look on her face, and I know it's too late.

"Now," her lips smack, "Walter Dupree knew how to treat a woman. There was this one time, I'll never forget it." She shakes her finger in the air and pauses. I press my lips together in a tight smile, patiently waiting for her to continue, even though I already know what she's going to say. Because I, too, shall never forget the story about Walter Dupree since I've heard it at least ten times. "We drove out to a cornfield. At first, I was shaking because we only had the lights from his Mustang shining on us. I was so scared. But I wasn't sure if it was from the monster begging to be freed from his dress slacks, or from being out in a cornfield late at night. There was no hiding anything from the pants boys wore back then. Those sagging britches they wear now are no fun. Only their boxers hanging from the back. Phooey. Who wants to see that mess? Show us the front or don't bother." Lois tilts her head at me. "What's wrong, child? You look a little peaked."

"Peaked?"

"Sick. Pale. Faint."

"I am feeling...peaked." The word feels weird on my tongue.

"Anyway, I'm from Missouri, and we're the Show-Me State. Show me what you've got to offer, I always say. Some of these boys want to gloat, whoop, and holler about what big men they are. Prove it. Show me. If you've got something to brag about—"

"I get it." I feel like I'm going to pass out. This woman is shameless.

"Walter Dupree didn't have to tell you he was packing, if you catch my drift. I could see the outline of that monster. And I, of course, was a lady. But that night, I let him do things to me that I don't think a two-bit whore would've done. My God. It was a full moon that night and we were wilder than rabbits in heat. Must've caused some kind of ruckus because I barely had time to get my pantyhose back on before we heard the sirens." Lois playfully smacks my arm. "I'm teasing. My mother had gotten worried I was out past curfew. She called the police to go look for me." She sighs. "Lost track of time during all the passion."

"Anyhoo," Lois begins putting away the rest of the books she's holding in her arms as she reminisces about her and Walter Dupree. "Before we knew it, we could see the lights. He took my hand and we ran through the cornfield. I laughed as we darted this way and that. The long stalks providing coverage. The leaves smacking us as we tried not to trip over loose corn husks on the ground. But we laughed. We laughed and laughed as we held on to each other's hands and ran through rows and rows."

My heart tightens as Lois idly rubs her fingers over her right palm as she remembers the feel of Walter's hand in hers. What it must be like to have such a beautiful memory. A night of passion and risks.

"The craziest thing was when we ended up coming full circle. The police cruiser was left unattended. Walter said we were already in trouble. They'd obviously spotted his car and knew we were there. I'll never forget my heart about to come out of my chest, but oh, I loved that man and the way he made me feel. We jumped in the car and dust flew everywhere as he spun it around the field. We drove all over that field as two more cop cars appeared, chasing us here and there. Walter and I whooped and hollered with the windows down, the wind throwing my hair into a mess, but I didn't have a care in the world. I sang out in laughter. Finally, Walter looked at me and said, 'Lois. You've got a reputation. I'm not letting you get in trouble. You're going to get out of here and go grab my car while they chase me. Go home, and say you were there the entire time.' So that's what I did. He'll always be the love of my life."

She always ends the story there. As per her usual routine, she then wanders away. I shake my head as I push my book cart farther down the aisle. At the sound of footsteps I turn, expecting to see Lois, but it's not her. I gasp, startled at the sight of Steffan looming over me.

"You!"

"So jumpy. You're like a little mouse."

I narrow my eyes and straighten my back. "And you're like a snake." I take a book and roughly shove it on the shelf. "What brings you slithering around here? Looking for your blonde friend?"

I hope not. We're closing soon, and Bryce will be waiting for me. Where's Lois? It's now registering that I'm alone with a potential murderer in the perfect location to do whatever he wants. Let's be honest, Lois isn't going to be able to reach me fast enough if I scream anyway. Nobody else is here. Nobody is coming. Nobody is safe. Lois and I are his next victims. If I whack him hard enough with a book, I might be able to get enough distance between us to call for help, find Lois, and hide until the proper authorities arrive and save us. I'm probably getting ahead of myself but I can't help it.

As I'm eyeing which book on my cart to use as my weapon of choice, Steffan steps around the cart, coming closer to me. "I can't figure out if you hate me so much because I've done something, or if it's that you want to fuck me."

"Wh-what?"

He's now invading my space. I step back until my back is pressed against the bookshelf, but Steffan doesn't stop. He places his hands on either side of my head against the books, and then places his foot between mine, spreading my legs farther apart.

"Excuse you!" I shove him back and hold a finger up. "How did you know Brother and Sister Myers?"

"I don't know. Guess I had you investigated."

"That's disturbing. What on earth for?"

"You've been hostile toward me. I deserve to know why."

My bottom lip trembles, but I force the words out. "I know what you deserve."

"Really? I'm intrigued." He leans down to where I feel the warmth from his cheek next to mine. I can smell his expensive cologne, mixed with some kind of spice. His voice drops to a whisper. "You gonna give me what I deserve?"

"You've missed class. Twice. Our professor is going to give us both a failing grade. One that I do not deserve, but you do."

When he doesn't respond, I make the mistake of looking up. Those intense, sapphire eyes are burning. Like the blue in a flame. My entire body is becoming hot. His mouth spreads into a slow smile. "You're not going to fail."

He brings his thumb to my bottom lip and begins tracing along the curve of my mouth. I'm at war with myself, wondering if I should jerk away from his touch, scream, or the most disturbing option, lick him. Who does this? Who acts like this? My God, he could be a murderer. If nothing else, he is acting very bold with me when I know he has a girlfriend. Plus, he doesn't even remember that we had sex. I'm afraid of what he might do to me. Worse, it's not only the fear that he could hurt me, but the risk of how alive he can make my body feel as well.

"You know what I think? I don't think you're worried about failing. A smart, nice girl like you? Nah. You know you won't fail. You won't allow that. You also won't allow yourself to admit that you're wet for me. That's what really has you all wound up, isn't it?"

"You're disgusting." He raises his eyebrows while still wearing that smug smile. I want to wipe it off his face, which is the only logical explanation for why I can't control my next words. "Why weren't you in class?"

"Worried I was with the blonde? I wasn't. But I've been busy."

"Busy filleting football players?"

That question successfully removes the smile from his face. His eyes turn glacial as his lips thin into a hard line and his jaw tics. "And what if I was?"

"Then I'd say you're sick."

"Oh, you have no idea. But you want to know the messed-up part that I bet really turns your stomach?" I meet his stare but say nothing. He presses his chest against mine, bringing his lips only a fraction from mine. "You still want me. I see it in your eyes." His fingers lightly skim down my neck to my collarbone. "The way your skin is getting flushed." I jump when I feel warm fingertips at the edge of my dress. "And I bet if I were to slide my hand up your dress, rip your panties off," his voice turns rough, "my fingers would find you fucking drenched."

I slap his hand, and then grab his wrist before he can bring it back to my leg. "Did you kill her?"

"Who the fuck is *her*?"

"That's right, you have a bad memory when it comes to people, huh?"

"What the fuck is that supposed to mean? Wait—the girl who was stabbed?"

"She was my roommate and friend." My eyes are burning, but I refuse to cry. I need to get this out. "And she should still be here."

"I'm sorry. I didn't do it. But I'm hoping to find out who did. Sure it wasn't you? I mean, you were her roommate. No forced entry. Heard you were the real religious type. Don't some of those hillbilly churches do something with snakes?"

"That's offensive. It's called snake-handling, and my church doesn't practice that. What about the guy your frat brother got into it with? I heard you made an example of him."

"Nope. But, again, I *will* find out who did it."

He didn't do it. I was convinced he had, but he's telling the truth. I don't know how I know—or even why I believe him—but I do. The conviction in his voice leaves no doubt that he's going to find out who the actual murderer is. He probably wants to know just as badly as me, since the murderer left Kasper's body as a present on his fraternity's house front porch. But who would kill somebody connected to me, and then kill another person somehow connected to Steffan? An alarming suspicion creeps into my mind.

He liked to cut. He once talked about snake-handling and faith. Both victims were cut numerous times and snakes were involved in both murders. Surely, *he* wouldn't have followed me here. That would be crazy, insane, and psychotic—even for *him*. Killing my roommate to teach me a lesson? Killing a football player and leaving him on Steffan's frat house porch to deliver—what? A warning? A message? Did Steffan taking something *he's* been obsessed with for years drive *him* mad, sending *him* into a rage where slicing his own skin wasn't enough? But there's no possible way for *him* to know. No. It's not *him*. I'm just being paranoid.

Steffan's nose lightly grazes mine. I'm hyperaware of how close his body is. My lips are familiar with how warm and strong his body is, and they crave to kiss the crook of his neck again. I swallow and try to control my breathing. I know he can feel my chest rising and falling against his. I'm making a fool of myself. And this is really awkward since my underwear is, in fact, drenched.

But before I can think any more about it, his lips are on mine. All my thoughts focus solely on him. His tongue massaging mine. His warm hand sinking into my hair and the other squeezing my hip as he fuses our bodies together.

Then I feel his thigh press firmly against me, right there between my legs, alleviating and worsening the ache. The pressure brings me only minor relief, but at least it's something. It's only that I want more. I want him. He guides my hips back and forth against him. As my body begins to relax, his hand moves from my side down to my bare leg. When I don't protest, he wastes no time bringing his hand back to my leg, but this time underneath my dress. Memories of our first time together flood my mind. I want it again. I've not had sex since him, and maybe it's because I've been waiting for him. Yet, he's obviously forgotten me.

Reality slams into me. He's not as tender, yet dominating, as he was that night either. Something is off, or I have put him on a pedestal and blown that night up to something more than what it was, since it was my first time. No matter the case, he has a girlfriend, he doesn't remember me, and something shady is still going on with him. Red flags galore. *Just my type...*

"No," I turn my face and place my hands on his chest, pushing him off me, "I have to go."

He steps back, licking his bottom lip. Steffan studies me and smiles. "What's the matter? Am I not as good as you imagined?" My heart stops at his words. But then he continues with a sneer. "You'd rather *watch* than participate? We can call Summer."

Mortified that he'd have the nerve to bring that up, it takes everything in me not to slap him. I refuse to let him get the best of me. Straightening my posture, I offer a smile as cruel as his. "I'm sorry, did I bruise your ego?"

"Broke my heart is more like it." *Sarcastic ass.*

"Wow. You're really a jerk. It's closing time, anyway, so you need to leave."

"But I haven't gotten your notes from class. Wouldn't want us to do poorly on that project now, would we?"

"I'll email you."

"What are you in such a hurry for? Can't wait to get back to your room, so you can double-click your mouse while thinking of me?"

What?

He takes his forefinger and moves it in rapid motions, invisibly clicking...*he can't be implying...oh gross!*

"You're very crude. I have a date tonight."

"I bet you do."

"I do!"

"With your battery-operated boyfriend?"

"No. He's actually waiting for me outside."

Steffan places his hands in his pockets and sucks in the side of his cheek, making his cheekbone more prominent. I hate how ridiculously hot he looks right now. Without another word, he turns on his heels and walks away.

The eerie feeling of being watched creeps up on me again. I feel a shiver as I listen and look around. I hurry down the end of the aisle, and I see Steffan standing by the door. Lois is by the front desk, probably shutting down the computers. Nobody else should be here at this time, but I still can't shake the feeling that I'm not alone.

The lights begin to turn off in half of the building. Quickly, I put the rest of the books on my cart away. I hear the sound of footsteps and call out, "Lois?"

Nothing.

Unease settles over me. I hurry up and work faster. I'm only being paranoid. I about have myself convinced of that fact until the sound of a squeaky wheel on a cart echoes in the room. I stop, the book in my hand paused midway in the air, while I try and listen harder. The sound grows louder, and the squeaking gets faster. I turn to see an empty book cart flying down the aisle toward me. I flatten myself against the shelf as much as I can as the two metal carts collide with a loud crash and a few of the books from my cart fall to the floor.

"Lois? Steffan?" My voice is uneven and higher than normal. There's no answer. I'm still pressed against the shelf, I allow my arms to rest on the top of books as my forehead leans against the cold, hard metal shelf. Something cold and scaly rubs along my arm. I jump back, but the feeling is still there, only worse... it's spreading.

I look down and scream at the top of my lungs as a tiny snake begins to wrap itself around my arm. Steffan's boots come pounding toward me.

"What happened?" I extend my arm, but no words leave my mouth as I open and close my lips.

Steffan takes the snake by the head and then carries it away. I follow him as he walks toward the front of the library and the main entrance. No way am I going to be left alone again. Lois looks up from the computer. "Gracious. I was hoping you'd get your hands on his snake, but I meant the one-eyed one."

Steffan grumbles, "This isn't mine. Not sure where she found it. But it didn't come from me."

Lois's bracelets jingle as she points at Steffan. "You remind me of my Walter. I'd be willing to bet you've got a bigger snake, too."

Steffan looks over his shoulder and winks. I need to remember to tell Lois we do not like Steffan or his one-eyed snake.

I follow him outside in a daze. Too much has just happened. I accused Steffan of murder, we made out, a creepy cart rammed into me, a snake slithered up my arm, and Lois openly stated that Steffan gives off big dick energy and reminds her of her 60s crush, Walter Dupree. Nope. No, no, no. I'm done for the rest of the night. I might lose my mind if one more thing happens.

Steffan releases the snake onto the grass. The fresh air helps ease the tension in my body. My lungs inhale as much as I can. Steffan walks up to me and then places his hands on my shoulders.

"It's okay. I'm going to go back inside to search the whole damn building."

Before I can thank him, a voice joins us. "Taylor? Oops, sorry. I hope I'm not too late."

Steffan's hands tighten on my shoulders, and he doesn't loosen his grip when I try to walk forward. His body has gone rigid behind me.

"How the fuck do you two know each other?" Steffan fumes.

CHAPTER SEVEN

Steffan

A rage I haven't felt since that night almost a year ago hums in my veins. My arm tightens around Taylor, as I push her back to shield her from Bryce. A smirk pulls at his lips when he sees what I'm doing. Taylor stiffens in my hold when my eyes meet hers accusingly. I hate that they know each other.

When she doesn't answer my question, I ask again, "How do you know him? Why is he waiting for you?"

She sighs and rolls her eyes, trying to move around me, but I block her. "I don't have to explain anything to you, Steffan. We have plans, so please move."

"No big deal, Steff," Bryce butts in, his southern drawl overly pronounced. "Taylor wants to go with me."

"Over my dead body, Van Doren," I practically growl. In my peripheral, I see Taylor's mouth part in surprise before an angry blush spreads across her cheeks. I make a show of my gaze dropping to Bryce's feet and trailing up his legs. "How's the peg working for you these days?"

The second my words hang in the air, Bryce's demeanor changes. The fake smile melts off his lips and his eyes blaze. The snake I knew was lurking underneath finally makes his appearance, and Taylor stops fighting against me.

"You're dead, Carmichael. You and your family will be nothing," he seethes, while I walk away, keeping Taylor at my back. There's a bang from behind us, and I glance back to see Bryce's fist smash against the library door. I smirk, knowing he was always such a hothead.

When we get to my car in the parking lot, I shuffle Taylor over to the passenger side, opening the door without a word. She sucks her lip between her teeth, and for a moment, I think she's going to refuse, but she gets in. I drive us across campus, ignoring the way she starts to fidget when she realizes I'm not bringing her back to the dorms. Instead, I pull the car into the parking spot in front of the fraternity house. My eyes roll when I see the yellow caution tape, as if the whole campus didn't already know where a body was found, and notice that other brothers are entering and exiting through one of the side doors.

"Come on," I tell Taylor, getting out and opening her door before she even has her belt unclipped.

"I don't think this is a good idea," she tells me, her eyes meeting mine warily.

I tilt my head. "Why? Because of Bryce?"

"No," her head shakes so fast, her hair swirls, "I just... I don't really know you, and too many strange things have been happening lately."

I glance again at the tape, mapping out the crime scene in front of our house. The campus asked that we shut down our fraternity for a while, but I refused. It isn't possible or feasible to move our whole operation somewhere else. We had hoped to catch whoever committed the murder on our security cameras, but there was a glitch, an interference with the equipment at that exact time, according to our tech guy. During the day, no one was around to check the cameras. We were all off at class, and some guys were doing their volunteer hours around town. Thankfully, with my father's connections, Lee was able to get information from the coroner that the murder occurred overnight between the hours of two and four a.m. Kasper was killed somewhere else and dragged to our front steps before being gutted. Whoever thinks they can mess with us is going to learn the hard way. We don't scare easily.

"Do you really think that I'd purposely mess up the front of my house if I was involved?"

Taylor's eyes fly to mine, and I see her mind moving over my words, contemplating. It bothers me that she doesn't automatically trust me about this. Sure, she followed me away from Bryce, but for some reason, now she's doubtful. My fingers latch onto her wrist, and I pull her behind me, through the side door and through our house. A few brothers stop to look, but when they get a glance at my face, everyone goes back to what they were doing. Taylor keeps quiet until we reach my room. "I'm not—"

Her words cut off when I swing my door open, only to find Summer, half-naked and looking through my drawers. "Can I help you with something?"

Summer jumps and moves her body in front of the drawer, trying to close it. Panic flies across her features as her eyes move over me before sliding to the girl standing beside me and where my hand is wrapped around Taylor's. "Who the hell is she?"

My brow lifts. "You're in my room without my consent and you're asking me about her?"

Summer stomps her heel-clad foot. "I was looking for an earring I thought I left here the other night."

"And how does that explain you being half-dressed? It doesn't matter. I didn't invite you here, and no one goes in my room without my consent, so who let you in?" I demand, my arms crossing over my chest.

Summer sputters, her face turning red. "Are you for real? You show up with some skank and have the nerve to question me? I think I'm the one who should be asking questions, Steffan!"

"I'm leaving," Taylor murmurs under her breath, before stepping away from me and fleeing downstairs. I watch as she almost collides with another girl, who is coming out of Lee's room. Taylor apologizes and keeps going. My eyes swing back to Summer, who crosses her arms smugly, and it's then that I feel my resolve snap.

"Get out." I level my glare at her, my tone icy.

"Steffan—"

"Get. Out." I step closer to her and see the way she flinches slightly from my words. I feel nothing as tears slide down her cheeks, or at the little show she makes of picking her dress up off the floor and running past me. I probably should care and stop her. But I don't. Someone let her into my room, and that is most definitely against the rules. Her little tantrum also sent Taylor running, and for some reason, that bothers me the most.

"Lee!" I call his name, knowing any minute he'll show up. It's just how he is. Reliable.

"Yeah?" He strolls in a few seconds later, a half-eaten apple in his hand.

"Who the fuck let Summer into the house?"

Lee squints, looking around my room before noticing one of the drawers of my dresser is ajar, right where Summer had been standing. "Two Scabs were the only ones here earlier."

"Who?" I ask, knowing it's a loaded question: who are they and do we really need them around?

"Branson and Anderson," Lee rattles off their names. "You can't kill them. The cops have already been to our house once this week, any more people dead or missing and it is going to start looking like we're guilty of something."

My eyes narrow, my mind spinning through all my options. Logically, I know Lee is right, yet my hands twitch to spill some blood. "They're on float duty. I don't want to see them until that float is up and running. They will not eat, sleep, or shit until it's perfect and ready for the drop."

Lee smirks and nods. "Branson! Anderson!" I hear his voice barking orders as he heads out of my room and downstairs.

I can finally breathe again. I step closer to the drawer Summer was just in and look inside. Nothing is missing, yet I can't stop the nagging feeling in the back of my mind that she wasn't being truthful. She had both earrings that night when she left here, that I know for sure. They were dangling and shaped like little hot pink hearts which are hard to forget. She was lying, but I don't know why. I rub my hand down my face before collapsing onto my bed. Taylor's face flashes in my mind, the feel of her lips against mine, and the way her body melted into me earlier causes heat to spread through my chest. There is something about her that calls to me. The fact that she was meeting Bryce tonight has me seeing red.

Bryce.

That fuck. I whip out my cell and shoot a message to Lee confirming that Van Doren is, in fact, back on campus. I need all the specifics. He and his threat to hurt my family is a death sentence.

"It's been three days," Lee murmurs as we walk toward where the judges' station is set up for the homecoming parade. "He's a fucking cockroach."

"We need to scare him out. Van Doren has weaknesses; he's more of a snake than anything else."

"I'd pay a visit to our good ol' friends at the football house, but after the incident with one of them being strung up by their innards between our pillars, they're giving me a wide berth these days." Lee shakes his head.

I chuckle. "Pussies. If we were going to take them out, we wouldn't be stupid enough to broadcast it all over campus."

"Some of them have taken one too many hits to the head," Lee quips back.

I shrug, my gaze scanning over the parade as it makes its way to the judges. After the fallout of Summer being in my room, Branson and Anderson completed the float in less than forty-eight hours. I think they knew their lives depended on it. I spot the contraption easily through the crowd, the blue petals from the papier-mâché roses dangling perfectly over the newly crowned homecoming queen. Once the float gets to the end of the parade, it will be intercepted by our suppliers and stocked up for next week's drop. Running guns and ammo can be easily accomplished; it's just a matter of how large the carriers need to be. In the past, we've transported in vehicles, kegs, and barrels. Due to the extra attention our fraternity is getting right now, though, it's a good thing we're able to use the inside of the float.

"Why does that chick look familiar?" Lee's head tilts as he examines our homecoming queen.

I shake my head. "Probably because you fucked her a few days ago."

"I did?" Lee turns to me, eyes blown.

It's the same girl Taylor ran into in the hallway after we found Summer in my room. "How the hell can you memorize every transaction that comes through for our orders, but you can't remember a girl from three days ago?"

Lee shrugs. "One means life and death for us."

We both grin and turn back to the parade. Brandon comes to stand with our group, and I wave him closer, so he can hear me over the marching band.

"I need details on Taylor's new roommate, Kali. I want to know everyone circling this girl."

"Can I ask why?" Brandon asks.

I give him a pat on the shoulder and say, "You can ask..."

"Yeah, all right. I'll see what Jerry and I can come up with."

There you go, buddy. Brandon wanders over to join a couple of our brothers who are laughing. Lee leans toward me, so only I can hear him.

"What's that about?"

"You don't think we should find out all we can about this girl? She just so happens to be in class with me, her roommate was murdered, and Bryce Van Doren was waiting for her after work. I want to know everything about her and everyone she's connected to."

"Interesting." A slow smile spreads across Lee's smug face.

"Shut it, Concord."

"Simple observation."

"Observe the fucking parade and see if you can find that piece of shit Van Doren."

"Okay, let me look for Taylor first. It might be easier to find him that way."

I force my face to remain stoic as a surge of anger courses through me. Van Doren better pray to God I never catch him with Taylor again.

"All right there, brother? Your knuckles are looking a little white."

I look down and force my fists to unclench. My eyes dart to Lee, who is eating this shit up.

"Not a fucking word." I warn him. Lee makes a grand gesture of holding his palms up in self-defense while his face feigns mock innocence. I look back out to the street and grumble, "Watch the fucking parade."

Our float has come to a stop in front of the judges' booth. My eyes scan the shiny white base, taking in the glitter-covered stem that arches halfway over the float and down to the neon pink sign that reads Thorn University Homecoming Queen. All in all, the guys didn't do a bad job of following Summer's orders.

"You smell that?" Lee asks suddenly. The minute he says it, the egg scent hits my nostrils.

I step forward, right when the bomb goes off. Papier-mâché, blood, and brain matter explode in the air, before cascading onto the crowd. People take off running, screams piercing the air. I can hear sirens a few seconds later, but my eyes don't leave the spot where our float is now on fire, engulfing what is left of the homecoming queen's body.

"No way," I hear Lee breathe out, and I follow him as he charges toward the destruction. We weave around the crowd, most people running away, and a few have their phones out, recording and live streaming everything. Right as we reach the barrier, the crowd separates, and I see them. Three black snakes spill out of the gaping hole of the float. My mind briefly wonders how they come out of this unscathed while a few of our pledges who had been on the float and the school queen are littered along Main Street.

"This wasn't an accident," I murmur, seeing Lee nod his head slightly. "We need to get out of here." We fall back into the crowd before I take out my cell phone and send a message to our suppliers, letting them know we need a new location. Then I send another text to my dad.

Me: Someone is targeting us.

CHAPTER EIGHT

Taylor

Sirens wail. Business owners rush out of their buildings with fire extinguishers. People are screaming and crying. The fear is palpable. Bodies push against me as they run past. Ash sprinkles down from the sky, along with shimmery pieces of paper. This feels more like a movie set, not reality. It can't be.

People around me are covered in debris. *Am I?* I take note of how grimy I feel. My hand trembles as I slowly pick off a bloody piece of metallic streamer, some lumped-together tissue paper, and what I'm praying are not parts of the homecoming queen from my shoulder. There's smoke and the smell of burnt flesh in the air. My heart is hammering in my chest and I'm *seeing* the carnage but for some reason, I can't process it. I feel *numb* other than the pounding in my chest and ears.

What happened? What in the hell just happened?

There's so much *red* everywhere...and on me. *It's paint.* I inhale a deep breath but it does nothing to calm my nerves because the stench only reminds me that this is real. The Delta Pi Theta float with our school's homecoming queen exploded.

My lips tremble and tears burn in my eyes but I still remain rooted in my spot. I'm watching and hearing all the chaos but I'm not seeing or listening. I'm in shock, or maybe finally having a mental breakdown. I feel something move next to my foot. A black snake slithers by and I my lips part but still no sound comes out. I finally find the will to move and slowly back away.

I turn my body away from the horrific scene. Two arms wrap around me, and I open my eyes to see it's Kali. I'd forgotten all about her being here with me.

"Let's get out of here," she tells me. I nod in agreement. As we start to walk, almost run, away, I get that prickly sensation again that I'm being watched. Stopping, my eyes scan over the chaos erupting around us.

That's when I see them. The black snakes slithering away from the float. My heart pounds against my chest. Smoke fills my lungs as I struggle to breathe and control the anxiety clawing at my throat. I look up from the snakes that are fleeing the chaos, and that's when I see him.

Steffan.

Could I have been so completely fooled? Is this his doing? Were his lies so convincing? The lips I kissed...were those lying, murderous lips? No. A serial killer. Oh my God. Did I have *sex* with a psychopath? I gave my virginity to him. The best night of my life was spent with...I can't even finish that thought.

How is it that I escaped one monster only to run into the arms of another...

When his eyes meet mine, I quickly turn my head and then begin walking faster. I need to put as much distance as possible between me and him. It takes Kali and me what seems like forever to finally get through the crowd. We're almost to Kali's car when someone calls out my name.

"Wait! Taylor! Hold up!"

Kali and I turn around to see Bryce catching up to us. I haven't spoken to him since we left him outside the library the other night. Steffan had been extremely hostile toward him, but why? I never got my answers, or any answers, for that matter. Then Bryce acted out by punching the building. I never expected such violence to come from him, which makes me wonder if the version I've witnessed has all been an act. Plus, Steffan's comment about his leg. After the mess I witnessed, I'd rather avoid both guys. Tragedies keep occurring since they've shown up in my life.

"Are you two all right?"

Kali laughs at him. "Are we all right? Are you serious with this shit? I picked chunks of the homecoming queen out of my hair. So no, I'm far from 'all right.' Nobody here is."

Bryce looks at me expectantly, but all I can do is shake my head. I'm trying hard to hold back the tears and to control my body's quivering. He keeps staring at me, and I want to scream at him to stop. Kali narrows her eyes at him and moves closer to my side. She takes my hand in hers. Walking backward, she pulls me with her toward the car.

"Wait a minute...didn't you date her?" Kali speaks very slowly and in a hushed tone. "The girl on the float...you two dated."

He barks out a short laugh. "Are you serious with this shit?" he throws her words back at her.

"Seems any girl who shows an interest in you or who dates you ends up with some really bad luck."

"Why are *you* so interested in my life? How do you even know this?"

Kali narrows her eyes. "Nice job of deflecting."

"Ya know what? I dated her, and so did half the football team."

"That's real mature, Bryce. You want to make her out to be some kind of slut to deflect. You're a real piece of shit. Get in the car, Taylor."

Bryce also showed interest in Ava. Not for very long, but they *were* hanging out. The snakes. He was at the library, too. He had that weird interaction with Steffan. He could even be connected to the murder at the frat house. I spin around and run to Kali's car. She unlocks the door with her remote. I can't get inside fast enough.

"Taylor! We need to talk! We need to go to the police together!" Bryce calls out to me, but I ignore it. Oh my God. It's just now coming to me. The murders didn't begin happening until Bryce came into the picture. It's him. It has to be. He's the one who is connected to everything.

Kali gets in the driver's seat, and then we hurry out of the parking lot, leaving that psychopath behind. Only then do I allow myself to break down in tears at what a fool I've been about so many people in my life.

Kali drives around the block a few times and then finally parks the car. She turns to me in her seat and asks, "How do you get beauty queen out of your hair?"

My eyes widen as I stare at her in shock. Then I laugh and cry when I see that her hair does have blood and debris in it. "We were probably supposed to give a statement or something back there."

"I do not feel like talking to the cops. I want to talk to Jack Daniels while soaking in a bubble bath. After I've rinsed all of this off of me thoroughly. I don't want soak in this shit."

"Thank you, Kali."

"For what?"

"For..." I smile at Kali and shake my head, "...I guess...just for your fucked-up sense of humor."

She clicks her tongue and winks. "I specialize in all forms of fuckery."

No surprise, the campus finally does shut down. Guess the third time was the charm. There's been one too many murders, and the school is making national headlines. The horror from the homecoming parade has now been coined as The Bloody Parade. Very fitting, since the pavement is stained red. My biggest fear is that it was only the opening ceremony to something far worse that's coming...

Neither Kali nor I wanted to return home to our parents, so we decided to rent a house—more like a shack—off-campus. It's not anything to brag about, since neither of us could afford much. Still, it's a much better option than returning home. As scary as it is to have a homicidal maniac with a snake fetish on the loose, I'm not ready to give up the independence I have here. Returning home means going back to my monotonous and strict life. My parents telling me who to be. *Him* always there reminding me who he thinks I am, or rather *wants* me to be. I'm still exploring myself. I can't spread my wings if they put me back in a cage, and that's where I'd be. I love my small town, my parents, and my church family, but I've not finished figuring out who I am without them.

Kali walks into the living room, wearing a long black t-shirt and aqua boy shorts. "Roomie, you know what you need?"

I close my psychology book and smile. "Do tell?"

"You need a tall, strong drink and a big, stiff dick."

Shocked by her words, I begin choking on my own spit. "Kali! Oh my—no."

"Are you kidding? You're so tense. I know this is all scary as fuck, but sitting here worrying about it isn't going to help. You've been on the same page for over ten minutes. I bet you still haven't read a single word. Let alcohol, a penis, and poor decisions take over for a night. I think you've earned it."

That sounds like a horrible idea. Listening to Kali would definitely classify as a poor decision. So I offer another alternative. "Or, hear me out..." I place my book on the coffee table and then turn my entire body to face her, in order to finish what I was about to say. "We eat a whole tub of cookie dough ice cream and watch the sappiest rom-coms we can find."

"A nice buzz and an orgasm, or lactose overload leading to high cholesterol, obesity, and diabetes? That's a tough one. I'll have to think about it." She walks over to the refrigerator and opens the door, pulling out a beer and yelling over her shoulder, "It's going to be a no for me." She closes the door and then turns to face me as she pops the top off her beer, yelling, "Cheers!" as she places the bottle to her lips and tips it up.

"Cheers to getting plastered by both booze and dudes?"

Kali sprays some of her beer. "Who says that? And it would be more like 'cheers to intoxication and fornication.' Now let's go get piss drunk and penised."

I tilt my head. "Penised? I think that would mean you have one."

"No, it means I got one...inside my vagina. But whatever, let's get schnockered and cockered." Kali holds her hands up. "Either way, let's get hammered and nailed. Drinks and dicks make us merry chicks. You get my point."

I roll off the couch, laughing so hard that my sides hurt. I'm not going out, but I appreciate her comedic relief. "How about we veg out in front of the television...you pick the movie or show, and we eat pizza and ice cream."

"Fine. But I get to pick the pizza toppings. No pineapple!" Well, that dampens things a bit. "Real quick, though. You and Steffan, what's the deal there?"

"I don't know. Do you think he's a part of all this?"

Kali lets out a dramatic sigh. "Honestly, Bryce seems to be the connection to everything. Plus, he has kind of a douchey name. Bryce Van Doren? Please. It's like his parents wanted him to become a serial killer."

My eyes bug out as I release a startled laugh. "Kali! This is serious. People around us are dying. Aren't you scared?"

"People around *you* are dying. I just came on the scene. Maybe you're the connection. Are you the one doing it?"

All the color drains from my face. "N-no. Do you seriously think I'm capable of those horrifying murders?"

Kali laughs. "Oh God, your face! No. But my life has been so fucking boring that rooming with a murderous bitch does sound like a thrill." Then, she mumbles, "My life is sad."

"Well, I'm not, so you'll have to settle for a B-I-T-C-H who's somehow connected to a killer."

She's quiet as her eyes study me, and I shrink under her gaze. Finally, she says, "You're a killer queen." Then after she takes a long drink, she bursts into song, singing, "Killer Queen" by Queen.

This girl is crazy, but I think she's exactly the kind of crazy I need when everything else in my life has been turned upside down.

CHAPTER NINE

Taylor

It's Monday. The worst day of the week, especially since I have psychology first thing in the morning. It's not lost on me that I'm taking a course that studies the human mind and how it works, with a guy I suspect could potentially be homicidal. But our classes have been switched to virtual, so I shouldn't have to face Steffan, again, other than through a computer screen.

I look at the square of my professor in poor lighting and the video slightly lagging as his voice comes through my computer speakers for one final announcement.

"Your class projects are past due. However, I am willing to give you an extension. If you're not comfortable or unable to meet with your partner in person, do so virtually."

Shoot. Immediately, my phone buzzes with a number I don't recognize.

Unknown: I think they're keeping the campus library open. Or we could meet at my house.

Obviously, Steffan somehow got my number. I add him to my contacts and then reply.

Me: Hello, Steffan. Virtual is fine with me. Let's set a time and I can send you a link.

Steffan: Library or my house.

Me: I have an obligation tonight.

Steffan: Yeah, to me.

Me: Hardly. I just started volunteering at Silver Creek Senior Living Center.

Steffan: Great. Those types of places always have meeting/game rooms. We can do the project there after you finish your "obligations."

Steffan: See you at 7. And you're welcome for the extension. I'm the one who convinced the professor. I'm sure you'll find a way to thank me ;)

Look at that. Not only is he bossy, but he's egotistical, as well. However, I will accept and be grateful for the extension. Let's just hope he isn't actually a psychopath. After all, he can't hurt me with an audience, right? Then again, the girl on the float had half the town witness her demise.

Despite Kali suggesting it's Bryce, I can't shake the feeling that Steffan is, in fact, dangerous. Unfortunately, my vagina didn't get the memo. The little hussy is practically vibrating at the sight of him. My whole body tingles, remembering his hard and solid frame pressed against mine in the library.

Those sapphire eyes are focused on each step I take toward him. I try not to let on, though, that I suspect him as the campus killer.

"It's five. I told you seven," I remind him when I reach him, standing in front of Silver Creek Senior Living Center.

"That's a helluva hello. Do you greet everyone so cheerfully and with such class?"

"What are you doing here?"

Steffan's lips rise on one side, giving me the sexiest crooked smile. "I'm here to volunteer. And then I have obligations to a beautiful, yet ill-mannered, fellow student. Those group projects are the worst, am I right?"

I narrow my eyes and release a frustrated huff. "You're the worst."

I walk past him and try to ignore his chuckling from behind me. At the front desk, I get my visitor's badge from Judy, who beams at Steffan.

"Taylor, you brought a friend. How nice." She smiles and gives me a not-so-subtle wink.

"*Isn't it nice...*" I purse my lips while responding with the fakest laugh possible. As if this couldn't get any more awkward, Lois appears.

"First the library, and now here? I'd say we've passed friendship. He's reached level three. Although, you two definitely need to find more exciting places to go and people to hang out with."

I'm about to scurry off and go find a nice lady to play blackjack with when I hear Steffan speaking to Lois. *Don't encourage her!* I scream in my head.

"Excuse me." He holds up a finger and then extends the rest of his fingers in a questioning gesture. "Level three?"

Lois leans her elbows on the desk. She pushes her breasts up and together to show off her cleavage in her V-cut blouse. *Oh, Lois.* She volunteers here in hopes of either finding a resident who has some life left, or a hot young doctor or nurse. Her words, not mine.

"In the beginning, it's all a game. Play it well, you'll reach the next level and new heights. You're at level three. When you reach level five, then you'll finally get to the real challenges and rewards."

"Challenge?"

"The challenge is you finally get a handful of titties, but you gotta handle them right, so she gets her reward, too. Then, if you're lucky, she'll let you go to the next level with new heights, and if you do it right, you'll both win the game."

Lois is talking to Steffan about getting a handful of my "titties." I'm done with this conversation. Time to go play cards. If there's a merciful God, I'll trip, hit my head, and forget that conversation ever happened.

After I left the most inappropriate conversation between a twenty-something-year-old college frat boy and a feisty sixty-seven-year-old cougar, I sat down to play a game of blackjack with Mrs. Chesterfield.

Our game is interrupted, though, by the commotion on the other side of the room. Steffan sits at a round table with five elderly ladies. All of them giggling, whooping, and hollering. Steffan yells playfully, "No, no, no. You are a hustler, Mrs. Manchester. Dirty. You're doing me dirty."

Lois appears beside me. "I'd gladly do him dirty."

"Lois," I scold.

"Even you can't deny that he's sex on legs. Or is it sex on a stick? I'd lick that man like a lollipop. A man like that...whew, he's an orgasm waiting to happen. If I thought I had a chance..." She visibly shivers. "You do, though. The way he looks at you is the way Walter Dupree looked at me." Her eyes narrow as she watches Steffan. "There's a familiarity there. He reminds me so much of my Walter."

"You and Walter never married. What if the same thing happens to me? Is it worth it?"

"I don't regret a single minute with Walter. And something tells me you won't look back and feel guilty for any time spent with that fella. If his dick is as big as Walter's and he knows how to use it, only then is it worth it, my sweet girl. See you in a few at the library!"

Lois shuffles away, leaving me with those deep and profound thoughts. And the reminder that I still have to go to work after this. I excuse myself from the table with Mrs. Chesterfield to use the restroom.

Before I can lock the stall door, it pushes against me. Steffan slides through and then shuts it, gliding the lock into place.

"What are you doing?" I hiss.

"What's with the evil glare?"

"You're in the women's bathroom and locking us in a stall together."

"Not now. Earlier."

I find courage that I didn't know I possessed. Maybe it's my annoyance that he keeps turning up that's bringing out this side of me. I don't know, but I'm feeling brave.

"Maybe I don't like *snakes*."

"Not even the one-eyed ones? Because that's a real shame. I was hoping to get to level six and introduce you two." Of all the egotistical things to say. Of course, I don't bother mentioning that his one-eyed snake and I have already met. Before I can tell him it's game over, he places a finger on my lips to stop me. "Let's play one game of blackjack together. I win, you sleep with me in my room. You win, I sleep in yours."

I burst out laughing in his face. "How do I win on either one of those?"

"Fine. You win, then all future projects will be conducted virtually. I win, and you're in my bed."

"Bed?"

"Yeah, for our slumber party."

His phone rings, making me jump. He chuckles and takes it out of his pocket. Steffan mumbles a few choice words and unlocks the bathroom stall.

"I have to leave, and I might not make it to the library for our project. But don't think I'm going to forget you owe me a game." He winks and then walks out the door.

I take a deep breath and shut the stall door, locking it back in place. The bathroom is quiet, but I get an eerie feeling that I'm not alone. While taking care of business, I lean forward and try to peek underneath the stalls. That's when I see a pair of black Chuck Taylors.

How long have they been in there? Why aren't they leaving? I don't even hear anything. My nerves and paranoia are getting the best of me, so I hurry up and finish, then unlock my stall and gently close the door. As quietly as possibly, I walk over to the sink. My anxiety spikes as soon as the water comes on. I hear the stall behind me unlock, so I dart out of the bathroom, not stopping until I'm out of the building and in my car, heading to work.

I drive to campus, not at all excited to be here. With all the recent murders, one would think the library would be closed down as well, but no, the library is still open for students to access. No gatherings are permitted, but if students need it for resources, it has to remain open.

I open my car door and listen. For what, I'm not sure, but my senses are on high alert. Once again, I try to be as quiet as possible as I shut it. I scan the library parking lot and the almost completely empty campus. It's creepy to see the place like this. Inhaling a deep breath, I make a run for the library entrance, racing up the steps and to the door. When I open it, I look behind me and feel foolish when I see nobody chasing me. Not a single person's around.

Get a grip, I scold myself. Lois hasn't made it here yet, so I go ahead and relieve the other worker and get busy. It's doubtful we even need more than one person this evening.

I grab a stack of returned books and then carry them in my arms to where they need to be placed back on the shelves. That being watched sensation begins crawling all over my skin again. *Stop it. It's simply because you're alone in a big library, with lots of book aisles for someone to be hiding, and the lighting in this place isn't exactly blinding.*

I don't usually give myself the best pep talks. No voice of confidence here. Swallowing down the lump of fear in my throat, I continue making my way through the stack of books. Out of nowhere, footsteps echo from behind me, so I stop walking, but so do they. I begin walking again, and then stop. Peeking through the shelves, I'm about to pee myself when I look back into a set of ocean-colored eyes.

My books fall to the floor, and as I bend down to pick them up, I hear the footsteps again. They don't stop this time.

"You scared the bejesus out of me," I grumble. Steffan doesn't speak. I squint and then shake my head. "Did you change clothes? What's with the dressy outfit?"

He ditched his casual clothes for navy blue slacks and a fitted dress shirt. Once again, he remains silent. He bends down, and I think he's come to help me pick up the books. Instead, he knocks the books from my hand and then gently pushes me down to the cold library tiled floors.

"Stef—"

He shakes his head no and places a finger to my lips. Removing his finger, he then puts it in front of his and whispers, "Ssshh."

My heart is having some serious palpitations, and I can feel it in other places as well. I inhale and notice the smell of tobacco. Not harsh smelling, but almost sweet. A hint of a woodsy smell as well. His eyes are slightly different from earlier today. There's a darkness to them, a burning and an intensity, and I find it difficult to stare into them for long. He's looking at me in such a sinful way that my chest feels like it might explode. Oh dear sweet Mary and Joseph, my ovaries might've just burst from the tension between us. It has me squeezing my legs together, feeling the wetness that is already gathering. This reminds me more of the Steffan from last Halloween night, and the anticipation of his kiss has me squirming beneath him.

Our lips are almost touching when we hear Lois. His face contorts in anger. *That's weird.* He usually always gives Lois his charming smile. Steffan helps me stand and then grabs all the books in jerky movements before spinning around and walking away.

"Hey!" I call out to him, but he doesn't turn around. One thing I do notice as he takes off in a power walk out of the library...he's wearing black Chuck Taylors.

Like in the bathroom. But it couldn't have been Steffan in there earlier. I watched him leave. Shaking my head at how ridiculous I'm being, I try to focus on getting through the rest of my shift, which is going to be difficult because I can't stop thinking about Steffan's intense eyes and wishing he would've kissed me. I wish I would've had the courage to lean forward and close the distance between us. I wonder if I let my desires take over and shut off my brain, how far I would have taken it...how far he would have let me take it. My mind wanders to thoughts of running my hands along his chest, down his torso, and gripping his thighs. I'd unbuckle his belt, undo his pants, and... I use my hands to fan my too warm cheeks.

What is it about this guy and libraries?

CHAPTER TEN

Steffan

One more set of blue and red lights flash when they pass me on the drive back to campus. Due to the recent murders, the campus has been crawling with uniforms ever since. I don't mind that classes have moved to being online for now, but I draw the line at the constant presence of police. Worse, they've tripled the number of officers, on and surrounding campus. Particularly, the reappearance of Investigator Rollands. Ever since last year and what went down with Bryce on Halloween, he has been a continuous thorn in my side, reappearing when anything happens on campus and visiting my house more than I would like. If Rollands was a stand-up guy, it wouldn't be a huge deal, but he's as slimy as Van Doren, and I wouldn't put it past him to be in the pockets of one of those rich prick's, who are trying to play big dog with their daddy's money. Rollands isn't on The Illicit's payroll, and he has plenty of questions about our fraternity that he never voices to us directly. I'll give him credit for at least having a shred of common sense in that area.

With all the extra attention from Rollands and the force lately, our operations are becoming a concern. My dad is not happy about it, The Illicit is not happy about it, and I can feel the pressure rolling off my back from the brothers and the new pledges, wondering what our next step will be. I've had to have too many conversations with my father, and Lee with his, making sure they know we can handle what is happening on campus.

"We should start our own investigation." Lee glances at me. "I don't trust these amateurs to know what they're doing. Remember how sloppy they handled Bryce's incident."

"That worked out in our favor, though," I remind him. "I don't trust Rollands either. It took three murders to get him out here. Something doesn't sit right in all of this."

"So far none of the cameras around campus have footage of any of the murders. The ones in the girls' dorms show nothing; ours had a glitch when the psycho strung Kasper up, and the cameras at the field house, where all the floats were kept before the parade, haven't worked since August. Whoever is doing this is acting during opportune times and knows the campus well," Suco adds to the conversation.

That's true. They're striking when the campus is nearly empty. Less traffic. Early morning. Late at night. Or they're studying their targets and waiting for the right moment to attack when they're around less populated areas.

"Let's keep looking," I tell them both. "They slipped up somewhere. We just have to find it."

Ever since The Bloody Parade, Suco's been brought further into the fold. It helps to show our fathers that we're a united front. We're working and handling this as a team. The Illicit head members are starting to get twitchy with the amount of attention that has been brought on our campus. With all the elites and mafia heirs in one place, we're all feeling the pressure. This could bring scrutiny to our illegal activities and dealings. One of us could be a potential target. Someone could use one of us as a way to get to our fathers. There's about fifty million ways this could all go fucking sideways.

The only silver lining to break up the chaos has been Taylor. This girl drives me crazy. If it hadn't been for the way her body melted into mine, or the fact that I saw her blown pupils when I bent down to kiss her, I would swear she was afraid of me. And maybe she should be. Dead bodies are lining up, and her room-mate was among them. The hot and cold game between us is fun. Despite what Taylor thinks, I enjoyed our time together today, even though she pretended to ignore me as she played blackjack and a few rounds of cards at the senior living center. It wouldn't have been horrible to hang out there and complete our assignments for class. I want to spend more time with her, so much that I'm tempted to go to the library, where I know she's working tonight. But I won't, since I have brotherhood business to take care of. That's the only thing keeping me from her tonight. And that's a first for me: wanting to hang out with a chick for more than a wham, bam, thank you, ma'am. Shit, I even want to know Taylor's last kiss, what she likes to do for fun, and what her family is like. She's different. I'm drawn to her sweetness, to the fierceness she has hiding behind her eyes. I've seen it, and I want to see it, again. The fact that she has no clue about The Illicit Brotherhood or Delta Pi Theta doesn't hurt either.

"Hey, Steff!" one of the brothers calls out as soon as I'm within eyesight of our house. I lift my chin in response. "Ahh—" He scratches the back of his head, glances around, then moves over to me. "Last time you said to let you know if Summer was here, but why did that change this week?"

"What?" My eyes narrow on him. Seriously, they have one job, and that is to make sure my room stays off-limits. "Summer is in my room? Fucking again?" I take off across the lawn and into the house, ignoring everyone who tries to stop me on the way. I can hear voices behind me, but I keep going.

My door is closed when I reach the hallway. I decide not to give her a heads-up, my hand wrapping around the knob and flinging the heavy, wooden door open. Summer jumps when it slams into the wall.

"Oh my God! Steffan!" She clutches her hands to her chest. "Are you insane?"

"What the hell are you doing here, Summer?" I storm into my room, my gaze sliding everywhere to see if anything looks like it's missing.

Her head tilts, her hair swishing with the motion. "You let me in."

My gaze narrows. "No, I told you not to be here unless I was here."

She crosses her arms. "Why? Are you bringing her here again?"

"Seriously?" I roll my eyes and chuckle. "It's none of your business who is here or not. I explicitly asked that you not be here."

"Steffan..." Her bottom lip slides out and tears gather in her eyes. "When you left, you said I could wait for you. Why are you being like this right now?"

"When?"

"What?" She looks confused, her cheeks turning pink. I can feel the hairs on the back of my neck rise.

"When did I leave and tell you that you could wait here?"

"Just a few minutes ago." Her answer is quiet, but it sends me into motion.

Soren. Goddammit.

"Go home," I snap at her, before stepping into the hallway. "Lee!" I call out, "we have a problem." He steps out of his room and follows me back down the stairs to where the cameras are feeding information from the hallways. Summer might be treacherous at times, but there is a possibility she thinks she saw and talked to me. After all, there is someone else with my exact face. And if he's here, some of these murders might be solved.

Thirty minutes later, a few of my fraternity brothers and I are gathered in my room, looking at the monitors, watching the camera feed from the past six hours. "What do you mean, you can't see faces?" I question Mickey, our top IT frat brother.

"It's weird, man," he shakes his head, "the cameras were fine all day, but right here..." He points to the screen, and all I see are legs. A pair of jean-clad ones, similar to my own and Summer's. "All of a sudden, the images are face down. It's like the cameras were moved or altered."

Fucking Soren. He'd know the procedures in this house, since he lived here too.

Lee meets my eyes from across the room, his brow raised. "All right, thanks, Mickey. You can go now."

Mickey looks between Lee and me before he stands up and leaves the room. I slide my phone out and send a message to my dad that we need to talk.

"Have you heard from him?"

Lee clears his throat. "Not since he left. Steff, if he's back..."

"I know." I open one of my old messages with Soren, my thumb hesitating over the letters. If Soren is here, it wouldn't make sense for him to be running around murdering people, or would it? No. I refuse to believe my brother would go that far, and if I accuse him of that, it will only push us further apart. "We need to wait before we jump to any conclusions." Lee opens his mouth to argue, but I pin him with my stare. "Messing around in our house is one thing. Multiple murders are another, and it's something Soren wouldn't do. He'd go after Bryce, not use all these scare tactics, and definitely not draw attention to our house by stringing up a corpse."

"You don't think Soren is holding a grudge?" Lee's brow lifts.

"With me, maybe, but never against the brotherhood, never against The Illicit. Despite what happened, Soren is just as dedicated as we both are. We have all shed blood out for The Illicit," I remind him, but loud enough for everyone else to hear me. I don't like him doubting my brother. None of them should be doubting him, even if they're not brave enough to voice their thoughts, I can read they're all thinking it. I'm loyal to Delta Pi Theta, but Soren is blood. They need to remember he is still a part of this fraternity, and he *is* part of an original family blood-line.

"We should keep this information to ourselves, then," Lee finally responds, his fingers running along his jaw while he thinks.

I spin my phone in my hand, contemplating how to handle my newest findings and what to share with my dad. He already wants to step in and interfere with the investigation on campus, but I've managed to talk him down, by convincing him that I can handle it. If he thinks Soren is back on campus, it might complicate things, and if he finds out I've been hiding this information from him, he'll become even more paranoid than he already is. "We hold on to it for now. Until Soren is caught in the act, we do not tell our families."

Lee's eyes flash. I've never asked him to lie to our fathers, but I know the ramifications this could have if it's not handled the right way. "While we're waiting, we should talk about the drop tonight. After the float exploded, everything was moved to the forensics lab. We were able to get in and grab what was left of the shipment, but the majority of it was wrecked. The guys junked it. I was able to smooth things out with the buyer, but they asked for double this time to make up for the losses. With that large of a shipment, we need a big cover."

"The Halloween party is the next big event on campus that we could use," Lee suggests.

I cringe, thinking about this year's Halloween party, even though it's weeks away. "Things have died down a little. Let's get the rest of the product out of the house tonight. We stick to the rest of the plan."

"How are we going to get it out?" Lee questions, pushing away from the wall and heading toward the door.

I shrug. "A few of the guys have bigger trucks. There's a football game tonight, so it wouldn't be too out of the ordinary for us to attend."

Lee snorts. "The whole campus is shut down because of a serial killer, but, sure, let's still have a football game."

"Welcome to Alabama." I laugh with him, before he leaves the room. I hear Lee barking orders to everyone, while I lean back and run my hands through my hair. There is not a lot of time left to get these guns out of the house. Our buyers are already questioning our ability to continue our work here with everything going on. Tension radiates in my shoulders just thinking about having to explain this to The Illicit if things don't go as planned. I can feel the pressure of my duties threatening to cave in on me. This needs to go right. They all need to know The Illicit Brotherhood is safe in my hands.

No more fuckups. I've got this. I need to remember who I am. I'm the president of the fraternity, but I'm next in line to be the leader of The Illicit Brotherhood. I *have* to maintain control over this situation. I can't lose it now.

One step at a time. I'll handle the deal. Find Soren, and figure out what's going on with him. Together, we'll figure out who is fucking with us and show them what happens when you mess with The Illicit. Death is coming for them. No one is safe from us.

The last bang of the celebratory fireworks dies away before I signal for our truck to break out of the line and away from the crowds. Our truck follows Lee's, winding over the back roads, away from campus. Dante, our connection to the buyers, had asked us to meet halfway between campus and his bar to make the exchange. I counted eight cops at the game running security, which meant eight others were out patrolling. Thankfully, the town was large enough that those on patrol would have to stick to the main roads. So far, the plan is working perfectly.

"Dante said to pull off when we reach the dirt road behind Rose Park," I tell one of the Scabs, who is driving us. His hands tighten on the wheel, but he manages to stay calm. I wouldn't say I'm impressed by him, but so far, he is doing better than expected. Scabs don't know all the details about these runs, but it's a good way to test their loyalty, to see how well they perform under pressure, and overall to see if they have what it takes to continue the pledge process.

We follow Lee a little bit longer, the truck bouncing lightly over the gravel and divots. A flash up ahead catches my eye, and I turn in my seat to look just as a set of bright headlights come at us. The Scab manages to floor it, and our back end is barely missed. "Everyone, stop!" I call out into the walkie-talkie. Dust flies in the air and tires screech. I reach into the back of my jeans and take out my Glock, before grabbing the silencer from the glove box. The Scab's eyes widen, but he manages to stay quiet. I jump from the truck, right as the unknown car behind us comes to a stop on our ass.

We're out in the middle of nowhere, so whoever is out here at this time of night is up to no good. That, or they're the ones who have been fucking with us and just signed their death sentence. There's also the possibility we've been betrayed by our business partners. Either way, my suspicion is raised. This car being here is not part of the plan, and I hate surprises.

I raise my weapon, just as Bryce steps out of the car, followed by five of his burly football buddies. My eyes fall to the leg he's stepping on lightly, before sweeping up to his face. Our eyes meet and I can see the hostility brewing in his gaze. He isn't here for a friendly chat, that much is obvious, and we have an important, time-sensitive job to complete. I'm tired of him pushing the boundaries, when he's clearly been told to stay off campus, but I have other work to do first.

"What do you want, Van Doren?" I question, keeping my tone bored.

He shrugs, looking smug. "Campus is shut down. We were asked by the Dean to report anyone who looked suspicious. A bunch of guys sneaking off campus, using the back roads, is something we should be investigating. No worries, I also reported it to law enforcement too."

My teeth clench, and a hundred different ways to kill him cross my mind. I hear Lee approaching before I see him. Bryce glances twice over my shoulder, so Jose must be with him. My brow rises and I watch as Bryce's face gets red and angry. We never treated him as a friend; we barely tolerated him. He now clearly sees the respect that is shown to Jose, who is only a pledge, but walks alongside with Lee.

"There's nothing in the rules that says we can't be out for a drive, or going into town for some food." Lee shrugs it off, his signature smile pulling at his lips. Out of the corner of my eye, I see Jose reach into his inside pocket. When his hand comes out again, there are silver rings on each finger.

"The rules say no one is to leave campus unless it's for a school function," one of Bryce's goons makes the grave mistake of talking back. My brow arches while I take him in. He's brave standing back there with his buddies. When everything goes down, and I fully intend to have a throwdown with Bryce at some point, Big Mouth there won't be forgotten. I'll see to that.

"I'm afraid he's right." Bryce smirks, thinking he's won something, and decides to take a step toward me until the barrel of my gun brushes his chest. "Besides, you aren't going to actually kill me, are you, Carmichael? Not without Daddy's permission."

I step back, holstering my gun. Bryce's posture relaxes, and I read the superiority that flashes in his gaze. He just never learns. My arm comes back before flying forward, my knuckles connecting with the side of his face. Bryce staggers back with blood running down his nose.

"You crazy fuck!" he yells, before charging at me and then grappling around my waist. Lee and Jose both fly into action, even a few of the Scabs, who were with us, join in on the brawl. But I only see Bryce. A year's worth of frustration, resentment, and anger boils out of me with every punch and kick I deliver. He manages to get me to the ground, and I swiftly roll him over. He flounders, his leg practically useless, before I deliver a shot to his ribs, and one more to his nose, effectively breaking it. Bryce yelps in pain, cupping his face. I climb off him and give one more kick, aiming for the side of his face. Fortunately for him, it's not a kill shot, but he does pass out.

Everyone still standing is all I care about. Blood and sweat pours from my brothers, but our enemies are all down. I walk over to the one who thought it wise to chime in. He is rolling onto his side.

"Hey, buddy," I say with mock friendliness. "What do the rules say about dickheads who harass other students? Where does that fall into your 'suspicious activity'? What'd your pal Bryce tell you?"

His lip curls and he spits out, "Fuck you, you rich prick. Think you're better than everybody. You're not going to get away with this."

He's more stupid than I originally suspected. "Is that a threat?" I look to Lee, "Did that sound like a threat?"

Lee crosses his arms. "That sounded like a threat. It's against the rules to threaten another student."

Jose nods with mock sincerity. "Verbal harassment is a serious offense. Name-calling. Threats."

"Yeah," Lee agrees. "Rich prick? I'm offended on Steffan's behalf."

"Fuck you, you rich prick, no less." Jose emphases a little too enthusiastically. "I'm appalled by this type of language and behavior. The football coach would be ashamed."

"Would he really?" Lee asks.

"Nah. But he'd still have to bench his ass if the school found out he was chasing students down dark back roads and picking fights."

I look back to our mouthy friend. "You picked the wrong fight."

I swing, but he blocks my hit, so instead, I use my other fist to land an uppercut under his chin. I'm still running on adrenaline and frustration. He's bigger than Bryce, and I welcome the challenge. I take a few steps back to allow him a moment to gather himself and stand. He circles around me, his eyes trying to watch me but also my brothers.

"Don't worry about them," I assure him, "you're all mine. They're not going to interfere."

"Even if I kick your ass?"

"Even then." I give him a half-hearted chuckle. This guy is full of jokes tonight. I've dealt with men that would make him piss his pants at the sight of them. He works out in the gym and takes care of his body, that's evident, but does he know how to use that muscle other than for plowing into another guy? Doubtful.

"Well, come on, then," he goads.

I give a taunting smile that causes his eyebrows to pull together in confusion. Then I shoot my fist out, hitting him between the eyes. I land a hard punch to his gut. When he doubles over, I grab his head and then knee him in the face, enjoying the satisfying crunch of his nose breaking. Bringing my hands together to make a single fist, I bring it down hard on his back, causing him to collapse on the ground.

"Don't worry about them. You can kick my ass. Come on, man. You're not still worried they're going to interfere, are you?"

He begins crying. "I'm sorry."

"What was that?"

"I'm sorry. Fuck, man. I'm sorry. You broke my goddam nose and, shit. I can't take any more," he grumbles out as he lies there in the fetal position, holding his nose with one hand, while the other is held up in a lame attempt to try and protect himself. For a moment, I think about what Soren would do. What my father would do. They'd probably take his tongue out. Maybe beat him unconscious. Drag him behind the truck all the way to campus.

Mercy is for the weak, but I believe it shows greater strength to be able to control one's anger. Which is what I'm going to do now.

"Let's get going," I tell the brothers, before spitting a wad of blood onto the dirt. Silently, they follow my order, and we make it back to the trucks. Bryce is going to continue to be a liability. Whether my dad wants to admit it or not, there is only so much leniency we can give the last Van Doren heir before he will pay with his life, just like his father. His actions tonight sealed his fate.

Whether he knows it or not, Bryce's grudge against us will eventually be the death of him.

CHAPTER ELEVEN

Taylor

A dark cloud of death and anxiety has blanketed the small town of Blue Rose. A beautiful, picturesque, southern college town has gone from being plucked out of a 50s sitcom, to resembling one of Dante's circles of hell.

My parents have been calling, begging me to return home. The reasonable and sane part of me knows they're right. It's dangerous here. But what they don't know about are the threats lurking right under their noses, waiting for me to return home...

Instead, I'll remain here. I'm invested in these murders, in finding the killer; one victim was my roommate, one was at the frat house of the guy I like, and what's worse, I fear I'm somehow connected. That should have me running back home with my tail between my legs, but that won't get Ava the justice she deserves. *Not sure how I'll get it for her if I'm dead, though.*

A part of me hates the fact that I know I'm also staying because of a certain messy blond-haired, blue-eyed boy. Gosh, how cliché. I'm apparently willing to die over some guy.

I haven't talked or seen Steffan much outside of class. We finished half of our project via video chat. I may have judged him too harshly, which I hate to admit. I wanted to ask him why he was so weird the last time I saw him at the library, but he didn't bring it up, so I didn't either. He seemed distracted on the video call, and I didn't want to get in his way or on his bad side. What Kali said still haunts me, whether it is true or not. I mean, his frat is intense. A secret society slash mafia type organization... I can't seriously be entertaining that thought. No way. *They never let anyone too close* she'd said. Has he kept a wall up around himself? Sure, they're secretive, but isn't that the point of the Greek social life? You're in an exclusive club, so to speak. But do pledges actually...disappear? How *do* they afford that mansion out in the woods? Maybe frat fees are ridiculously expensive. Or they have generous alumni that donate every year. Kali's in my head with all those over-the-top rumors. I'm ashamed of myself for entertaining such nonsense. Mama always said idle gossip were the Devil's tools, poisoning the mind and making it a place for Satan's workshop. She was right. All of that is just too far-fetched to be the truth.

A cool breeze tosses my hair as I exit my car on the street in front of my *very* humble home. Goosebumps break out over my arms and the back of neck as I get that unsettling feeling again. I used to think I was being paranoid, but the bodies are stacking up around me so, yeah, my feelings seem justified.

I keep my key wedged between my fingers, in case I need a weapon, while I hurry to my front door. I unlock it and then shove it open, just enough for me to squeeze through. I slam it shut and then lock it immediately. My forehead falls against the door with a thud. When the heart palpitations subside, I push myself off the door.

Kali isn't going to be home for another hour. The silence is eerie, and there are shadows that appear to be dancing on the walls and ceiling, so I decide to go through the house and turn on every single light. No matter how ridiculous I'm being, it calms me down.

When I get to the bathroom, I pause in the doorway. *Did Kali not drain her bath water?* As I reach for the light switch, I frown at the tub full of darkened water that seems to be moving.

A scream rips through my throat as the room illuminates to reveal hundreds of slithering black snakes in the tub. One of the snakes peeks its head over the tub and looks right at me as its pitched-fork tongue dances at me.

A few more glide along the rim of the tub as others weave over and under each other. Their motions are so fluid, I'd almost consider it beautiful, if I wasn't so horrified at discovering them in my bathroom.

My scream this time comes out as more of a strangled cry as I quickly step out of the doorway, closing the door behind me. I shake my hands, my entire body trembling as I try to get rid of the feeling that snakes are slithering all over me.

All of a sudden, a gripping fear takes hold of me and immediately stops my hysterics. Oh. My. God. If the snakes are here, does that mean the killer is too? *Was there a body underneath them?*

I run to the kitchen and grab a knife. I lower myself to the floor, keeping my weapon in front of me, ready to slash anyone who comes near me. My phone rings, startling me so much that I jump in place, releasing something between a cry and scream, and I almost drop the knife.

"*Dammit,*" I cry and wipe the snot from my nose with the back of my hand. My phone rings again and I'm terrified that I've done everything but wave a light to let the killer know exactly where I am. I'll never make fun of the victims in horror movies again. *That is if I survive.* I grab my phone from my pocket and switch it to silent. Answering it, I place it to my ear as my eyes scan for any movement.

"Hey, girl! I've got to work later. Someone called in so I'm working a double."

"Kali," I whisper, "th-the snakes. The killer. He or she has been in *our* house. Or maybe," I hiccup and release another cry. "Or maybe," I repeat and gulp, "they're still *here*."

"What? What are you saying?"

"Snakes!" I wail and then cover my mouth to shush myself. *I'm an idiot and I'm going to die.* "Kali, there are *snakes* in the bathtub." My voice gets caught in my throat. I can't hold it together any longer. The phone drops from my hand, and I hug myself, sticking my head between my legs in defeat.

I don't know how much time passes, but my body is stiff from being so tense. Inhaling a deep breath, I dig deep within myself to gather what little dignity I have left. I won't sit here another second trembling in a puddle of my own tears. I can't take it anymore. Everyone has their breaking point, and I've reached mine. Walking into a dark house with a bathtub full of snakes would drive anyone to the brink of insanity. That was the last straw for me. I've lived through so much these last few weeks and it's finally caught up to me. I bow my head once more and whisper, "Dear God, please give me courage. Fill me with your light and protect me." As I continue praying, a single tear slides down my cheek, and I'm determined that'll be the last one.

I pick up my phone to see I'm still connected with Kali. It's been over fifteen minutes.

"Hello?"

"JESUS CHRIST! You scared the shit out of me!"

I sniffle then wipe my nose on my sleeve. "Don't take the Lord's name in vain."

"I'm already going to hell for when I kill you for giving me the biggest fucking heart attack. You call me crying, and then somewhere in your hysteria mention killer snakes, then you fucking ghost me!"

"I did not say killer snakes. I said the killer left snakes." I stand on shaky legs and rub my clammy hands together. Anger begins to replace my anxiousness. I'm so over being scared, timid, and feeling weak. I hate it.

I can't live this way anymore.

"I'm on my way, okay? I had to tell my boss, and I borrowed someone else's phone to call the police. I didn't want to hang up in case you said something, or I heard something. Fuck, I don't know. But I'm in the car now...about fifteen minutes and I'll be there. The police should arrive any second."

"Okay. Thank you. You're a really good friend."

Kali releases a shocked laugh. "If someone not letting you die or get a snake shoved in your corpse are your standards, maybe you need to raise the bar a little. Just hold on a little longer, and when I get there, I'll shove a snake up this psycho's ass."

Kali's words fuel my courage. *Yeah, that's right. We're going to shove those snakes up this psycho's ass.* The phone still to my ear and the blade of my knife extended, I ease one foot in front of the other. "Come out! Here I am! You want me, well, now's your chance!"

I hear Kali yelling my name through the phone, but I ignore her. A part of me doubts the killer is still even here.

"Come get your snakes, and all of you get the hell outta here!" I don't hear anything, and they probably would've already attacked me by now. Was this simply another scare tactic? Kali continues to yell through the phone, and knowing she's there means a lot. Knowing the police are on their way means even more. I take a more confident step and call out, "I'm going to shove those snakes up your psycho ass!"

A door creaking has me turning to the right. *Shit!* I hear heavy footfalls. My hand trembles, but I remain rooted to my spot with the knife braced in front of me. Then sirens blare as bright lights shine through the cracks of the blinds. *Thank you, Jesus.* Fists begin pounding on the front door.

I think I hear the back door shut, but I can't be certain over all the commotion out front. I ramble into the phone, "Kali, there's commotion everywhere and I don't know what to do or where to turn. Also, I threatened to shove a snake up someone's ass but honestly, that's gross and cruel to the snake."

"Police!" comes from the front door, followed by another bang. I rush to unlock the door and throw it open. Men in uniform come inside and one calls out behind him, "Check the back! Around back!"

Without thought, I follow an officer to the back of the house, because I *have* to know. I *have* to see who is behind all this, but I see nothing. There's only the sound of crickets and leaves blowing in the wind. Men in uniform call out to each other as they search. Some going in the house while others investigate the perimeter. Before I walk inside, I notice a pack of cigarettes. I bend down to retrieve them. Kali and I don't smoke. In fact, I don't know anyone who does. I don't recognize the brand—not that I would—but for whatever reason, I open the flap and sniff.

I know that smell. Memories from last year flood my mind.

Halloween night. A mask. And the bluest eyes. He had this faint scent on him then, but I haven't smelled it since.

What was Steffan doing here? Did he leave the snakes? Is he...

Once again, my mind is running crazy and thinking the worst of Steffan.

I didn't tell the police my suspicion of who the killer might be, but I plan to. For whatever idiotic and reckless reason, I want to confront him myself. I gave him my virginity, so maybe I won't get murdered, right? Or maybe he likes to play with his prey before he strikes?

I call Steffan under the ruse that I want to discuss the theme for our project. When in reality, for once, academics is the furthest thing from my mind.

"I'm a little surprised you're wanting to meet in person." *You and me both.*

"We're partners, right?" *Establish trust.*

There's a pause. Did I push too much? I made it too obvious that I'm trying to trap him. He's on to me. Of course he is. If he's been outsmarting the police all this time, did I honestly think a few psychology courses would make me qualified to manipulate him?

"Partners," he draws the word out like he's testing it out. "Come to the frat house." *Great. Just great.*

"The Devil's lair. Fabulous."

He bursts out laughing and asks, "Hold up. Did you just call it...*the Devil's lair?*"

"Yeah. I did. I'm sorry. That came out...wrong. I feel bad now. That wasn't fair to say." I'm not one hundred percent positive he's a mass murderer. My parents were always judgy, and I really don't want to be *that* person. So what if frat houses are stereotyped as places for orgies, drinking, drugs, and sins of all nature. Didn't I willingly flock to a party at this house last year on Halloween? I'm going to go observe, investigate, and try maintain an unbiased opinion.

"No, no. Don't take it back now. Please." His voice turns into a hushed whisper in my ear, "Come to my lair." *Click.* I stare at the screen of my phone, where the call has ended. That shouldn't have sounded so hot. But it did.

I knock on the oversized double doors. A gorgeous guy with wavy black hair opens it and stands before me with a bored expression on his face.

"Can I help you?"

Another guy walks behind him and laughs. "She must be lost."

I narrow my eyes and force a tight-lipped smile. *Jerks. Or more like Satan's minions, if we're keeping with the Devil's lair theme.* Don't be *that* person. Don't come off goody-goody and judgmental, even if they are jerk faces. I turn my smile up a notch and force some enthusiasm into my voice. "Steffan invited me over."

Shock crosses their face, which would be funny if I wasn't slightly concerned for their health. They're turning awfully pale.

"Send her up to my room," a voice commands from somewhere in the house. The two step aside to make room for me to pass. *This is so dramatic.* It's not like I haven't been here before. Although, last time, I did arrive with Steffan. Maybe they think I was a one-and-done and are just shocked to see me again? As I enter the mansion, I can't help but admire how it's modern with renovations, yet still maintains its old-world charm. There's a dazzling chandelier, a wide wooden staircase with red carpet, and a giant fireplace off to the side. I can also hear a game of pool being played in the other room. I bet they have someone come and keep their ultimate bachelor pad clean. I'm surprised there isn't a maid scurrying around or a butler. More likely, they'd have someone in a risqué naughty maid costume to do their cleaning. Then again, who's to say they don't? I'll add that to my list of things to inquire about. As I'm taking everything in and coming up with my wild theories, all the guys are eyeing me with curiosity. I'm sure I'm not the typical female visitor, but surely some of them have hired tutors before. It can't be *that* uncommon to have someone who's not all plastic and cosmetic prancing through their house.

I walk over to the grand staircase where Steffan calls out, "In here."

As I climb the stairs, I stop halfway and turn back to look at my audience, who continue to watch unashamed. "Stop staring. It's creepy...and weird."

A few snicker and look away, while some seem like they couldn't care less. *Well, I tried.* I make it to the top and then follow the long hallway. I notice photos along the wall. One photo, in particular, has me coming to an abrupt halt.

No effing way.

It's an old portrait of an extremely handsome young man with black curly hair and the darkest eyes. He reminds me of someone that I can't quite place, but that's not why I'm about to pee myself.

Underneath the portrait, it reads *Walter Dupree.*

I rush into Steffan's room, slamming his door in the process. Before I can say a word, he stands from his chair, putting his hands in the pockets of his slacks.

"You're probably the first person to ever barge in my room and have the nerve to slam my door."

Probably. But I'm running on pure adrenaline. I should also be taking into consideration that I came here to confront him about being a serial killer. He would've already killed me by now if he was going to. Plus, I *need* to know if that's Lois's guy. *The* Walter Dupree.

"We'll swing back to that. First, do y'all have a maid that cleans this place?"

"Scabs do it."

"What's a...*Scab*? Like...as in a sore...scab?"

"Pledges. We call them Scabs. They clean."

Huh. There goes the naughty maid theory...unless they force them to dress in costumes. *Possibly.* Not going to rule that out just yet. "Since you're a member, are you a Scar?"

"President."

"*Oh.* The president. Your Honor." His eyes darken as he watches me. My playfulness evaporates as I feel the weight of his stare. A spark begins to grow, sending heat throughout my entire body, but I decide I need to extinguish that fire if I plan to get any answers. I remember my surprise in the hallway. "That Walter Dupree guy in the picture, he has the same name as the guy Lois has been talking to me about for the past year. What happened to him? Was Walter part of this fraternity?"

Steffan stares me dead in the eye and says, "No."

"Then why—"

"He *was* the fraternity. Not part of it. He ruled it. He was the very first one.

"Walter Dupree created all of this. He was a mixed-race man who was never going to get ahead because of his ethnicity. He didn't belong to either side of his parents' society, so he made his *own*. An organization made up of him, a few Italians, African-Americans, Spaniards, Mexicans, Irish, Cajuns, and other mixed races who didn't feel like they belonged anywhere. It was a bunch of guys wanting more for their families. Men willing to do *anything* to see a better future for their children. Men willing to take matters into their own hands."

The way he's watching me makes me feel like he's looking for something. My reaction? Is this a test? Because it sure feels like it.

His mouth forms a faint smile before he bites his bottom lip. He looks ridiculously sexy right now, even though he is obviously talking about murder. It doesn't escape me that that's the topic I originally came here to discuss with him.

"That's why our motto translates to *danger is sweet*. And we use the Greek letter, *Theta*. At one time, it was the symbol for death. But that was a long time ago, of course."

"We all have a dark history," I whisper.

"Some of us are still living in our dark past." Steffan's voice is hard, but his eyes hold so much vulnerability. I want to ask what dark past is he still living, but I try to offer him comfort instead.

"Then come join us in the now. The future looks bright from here."

He releases a humorless chuckle. "You mean a future with you? That wouldn't make you very bright. Definitely not the wisest choice."

My eyebrows pull together. I cross my arms and chew on the inside of my cheek. After a beat, I ask, "Are you implying that I'm dumb."

"Of course not. I'm stating that you make poor choices."

"Any evidence to back that statement?"

With three long strides, Steffan stands directly in front of me. "You entering this room, for one." He cups the back of my neck. "And you letting me do this, for another." His lips touch mine.

They're gentle and soft. He caresses my mouth slowly, his hand on my neck keeping us firmly together as his other hand guides our bodies toward the bed.

"Wait." I pull back before I can be persuaded to lie down.

"I guess I won't make it to—what did Lois call it? Level three?"

"You're not going to complete any level tonight."

"But the game's not over?"

I think about it. Is it? I guess it all depends on his answers tonight. What scares me most is not if he is the one behind the murders, but the fact that I don't think my body will care either way. I'm horrified that I might very well still let him have me and worry about the consequences afterward. But what if that means me wearing a toe tag?

"The game isn't over yet."

"Yet," he repeats with a cocked brow.

"There were snakes in my bathtub."

All playfulness leaves his face. His eyes scare me with how dark and stormy they turn. "When?"

"Last night."

"Are you okay? Did you see anyone?"

His hands clamp down on my arms almost painfully, but I don't think he realizes it. I can feel the anger rolling off him, his body vibrating with barely contained rage.

I'm on an insane rollercoaster of doubt. It is him; it isn't him. And now I'm back to it's not him.

I know it in my heart, but also, seeing the fear and anger in his eyes convinces me. "No," I answer him. "I called the police."

"Good." He releases me and paces the room. He runs a hand through his hair and growls.

He stops and turns to me. "You're staying here. No room for argument. This sick fuck knows where you live. I'll chain you to my bed if I have to."

"You barely know me." He gives me a *really* look. "Okay, fine. But only if my roommate can come too."

"Done. But she's not staying in my room."

"And I am?"

"Yes. I can protect you better."

"I bet you can. This isn't about completing the next level, is it?"

"Nope. But I might get a chance to score bonus points."

"If this is all a game, don't let me lose so bad I'll never be able to play again."

He kisses my forehead. "Same. Don't let me fall in love."

Why did he say that? It's a moment before he pulls away, but when he does, a sad look crosses his face. His fingers flex around my arm. Our foreheads touch, and in a rough voice, he says, "I've pledged my loyalty to the...brotherhood. It's... We're not like the other fraternities." Why did he pause? Did he start to say another name?

"Are y'all vampires?" I try to joke.

"Worse, I'm afraid. Love will not end well for either of us. I don't want you to think this could go past a college romance. My future is mapped out. It's out of my hands."

"And here you were just telling me that you're part of an organization whose legacy was built on taking their future into their own hands."

His eyes widen in surprise. Before he can answer, there's a knock at the door.

"Go away," he commands, while not taking his eyes off me.

"The fuck I will! I heard you have a *guest*."

"Dammit to hell. Can nobody do anything right around here?" He grumbles as he charges over to the door. When he opens it, there stands the blonde. My heart tightens at the sight, right before it hardens. I cannot with this guy. He almost had me believing him. *Duh.* How could I be so stupid to forget he has a girlfriend?

Summer shakes her head. She seems to be in as much disbelief as me. "Really? Wow. You move fast. I bet your dick hasn't even had time to dry from my last orgasm!"

She leans around him with a fake smile spread wide across her face. "Hope you haven't sucked his dick yet, honey. Unless you like the taste of pussy."

Steffan shoves her out the door and shuts it behind him. *Oh my gosh.* My heart is cracking and crumbling to ash. Screw this. I wanted to find my mystery lover for so long, but now I wish I never had. I liked who I thought he was. The fantasy I built up in my head. But like that fantasy, that guy isn't real. Instead, he is a cheater. *And possibly a freakin' murderer.*

I open the door and shove past them. Before I get too far, I turn around and tell him, "I don't think anyone has to worry about you falling in love. I'm not so sure you're capable of it."

I think I see a flicker of pain in his eyes, but I've imagined things before. He doesn't stop me as I hurry down the stairs and out the door.

I drive to the library. I'm too worked up to go home and do nothing but think of Steffan. I'm locking my car, lost in self-pity, when I hear a piercing scream. I turn around to see a commotion down the street. I take off in a hard run, fearing the worst, but wanting to be there if someone needs help. It's at the other frat house, the one Bryce and all the football players are part of.

There's a guy in the driver's seat of a big truck. The truck bed is full of crates, and some are open and filled with guns. The side of the truck has the word *traitor* spray-painted across it. I stare at the guy, trying to figure out his cause of death. But then I see his eyes move. A tear trails down, but he remains immobile. I ease through the crowd as everyone stares but doesn't offer to help. A few people are crying and covering their mouths. Others are on their phones, shouting the location and pleading for help to hurry.

Finally, I see it.

His hands are zip-tied to the steering wheel. It appears his lips have been sown together. And there, attached to the steering wheel, with a string tied to it, is a gun aimed directly at his head. The reason nobody is helping is the gun is also tied to the truck door. Nobody knows how to get him out without setting it off.

On the hood is a football helmet. Much to everyone's horror, a black snake pokes its head out as it slithers toward the open driver's side window. We all listen to the struggles and muffled screams of the trapped guy as the snake goes up his arm.

This is the work of the murderer, which means Steffan is innocent. It's not him. He couldn't have done this because I was just with him. All this time I've been wrong about him, yet I'm not completely surprised by his innocence in all this. Trauma from my previous relationship had me automatically jumping to the worst-case scenario. Not anymore. Life is way too short. Steffan could be next. I could be next. This stupid bickering and back-and-forth game needs to stop.

He's not a killer, but there's still one out there and the latest victim is struggling for their life in front of all these onlookers. I send a silent prayer to God to help us all. I've never felt so help-less and terrified in my life as I rack my brain for what to do. How can I help? What can I do that's not already being done?

A guy who looks vaguely familiar comes running through the crowd, shoving people in his haste. "Jerry!" Tears stream down his face as he takes in the sight. "Don't move! We'll get it out of there!" He scans the area frantically. "Fucking get me something to pull that damn thing out. Do something, assholes!"

Everyone yells in panic as they search the ground for a stick or something to grab the snake with. However, one stick won't be enough. More snakes slither out of the crates and enter the cab of the truck. Black snakes are crawling all over. When one finally reaches his face, I watch as his scream finally rips the stitches, and his bloody lips separate.

It all happens so fast. My body is spun around, and my head is cradled into a warm, solid chest. The guy in the truck's shriek is followed by the sound of a gunshot. There's an eerie silence of everyone's shock before they all erupt into wails of terror. The worst sound is the guy's cry of the victim's name. *"Jerry! God no. Jerry. WHY?!"*

I smell the familiar scent of sweet tobacco and woods, just like the cigarettes I found outside my house, right before allow-ing my mentally and emotionally exhausted mind to give in to the darkness.

"Tay." He sighs against my lips. "My control is so fragile when it comes you. My will to refuse sin is crumbling. I'm crazy about you. I love you so much that it scares me. My father knows."

"Brother Myers?"

"Yes. He—" He pauses and looks so ashamed. I reach out to cup his cheek. He's so strong, even for a teenager. He looks like

a man. It's heartbreaking to see him look so defeated. I don't understand.

"Tell me. Hey, I love you. Nothing you could say or do will change that."

"Do you promise? Do you mean that, Tay? Your love, is it unconditional and pure?"

"Yes." And I mean it.

"Brother Myers, my father, reminds me that my real parents were the worst kinds of sinners. Their saving grace was giving me to him and Sister Myers. He said I need to work extra hard because while we are all sinners, I have the blood of the debased. Wickedness of the most unholy courses through these veins." He holds his wrists out before me. "Sometimes I feel it take over. Last night, he caught me. When the urge took over and I fell to my immoral weakness."

"He caught you? How?"

"I was touching myself...while..." He turns his face away from me.

"It's okay! Hey. Tell me." The urge to take away his pain is so strong. I've never known anyone with a more gentle heart. Why is he so tormented?

"My perverse thoughts took hold of me. I touched myself while staring at a photo of you. Father walked into my room. I'm sorry. I'm so sorry." He wraps his arms around me and I hold him tightly. I rub his back as I whisper words of reassurance.

"He struck me across the face. I felt my tainted blood drip from my nose. But the urge to sin was gone. Now I know how to control it, Tay." I watch in horror as he releases me to pull out a razor blade. "I will not fall victim to the sins of my parents. Though their blood flows in these veins." He presses the blade against his skin.

"Stop. You're hurting yourself. Don't do this."

Tears fill my eyes while his turn angry. "You promised. Our love is pure, Tay."

My dream changes. It's no longer the memory of *him* sharing his secret with me. It's Halloween. I'm dressed as a mouse again, and Steffan has his back to me. I call out his name, and he turns around wearing his skull mask.

"Steffan! I'm so sorry. I've been going back and forth. Full of doubt and my own insecurities. I know you're not the killer. I think I've known all along. I also know that I haven't stopped thinking about you since Halloween. I love you."

He tilts his head and stares at me. But something is off. He raises the mask, and I scream. It's not Steffan. It's him! "But you promised to love me. ME! You harlot! Wickedness flows through your veins! You need to be washed in the blood..."

He steps aside and there's Steffan's dead body on the ground. "No! No! I love him! What have you done? No!"

"Taylor!" Kali screams, and I jolt upward. I'm in my bed. How did I get back here? The guy in the truck... I felt Steffan hold me, or I thought... I fainted. I vaguely remember coming to and Kali helping me out of her car and into our house. I look to my window and notice it's dark outside.

"I'm sorry. I—I must've had a nightmare. A memory mixed with a horrible nightmare."

"You were screaming you love someone."

"I'm in love with Steffan Carmichael." No denying it. It's a relief to finally confess it.

"Yeah, that is a nightmare," Kali mumbles, but I see the teasing in her eyes.

"The last time I was in love with someone, it was scary," I confess.

"The biggest highs come with conquering fears."

It's time for me to stop letting my anxieties and past trauma rule my life. I'm going to allow myself to see what could happen between Steffan and me. When my parents ask me to visit, I'm going to go and stop running from my past. And I'm going to figure out who murdered Ava and left snakes in my bathtub.

CHAPTER TWELVE

Steffan

My head throbs in time to the beat of the base that is pulsing throughout the house. That fucker had Taylor in his arms. *In his fucking arms.* The sight of Soren holding Taylor is still playing on repeat in my mind. The only reason she got away from me, or rather left me in my room, was because of Summer. I want to rip my brother to shreds. I chased after Taylor to the library, but I was too late. She was already running toward the scene before I even had my truck turned off. That's when I saw someone else die, and then her with *him*.

I didn't get a chance to intervene, though. I caught sight of Brandon being pulled away from the truck. It was his boyfriend, Jerry, who died. Brandon is beyond torn up over this. He wants vengeance. If it was up to him, he'd turn this entire town into a bloody massacre to find out who killed Jerry.

Jerry's body was sent back home, and I gave Brandon permission to leave and be with his family. Making sure Brandon gets help for his mental health has been my primary concern of late. I've already got enough loose cannons at the moment. Before he left, he looked at me with dead eyes and said, "He was digging about your girl. Think she's the reason he's dead? Tell me, Carmichael."

Carmichael. Not President. Not Steffan. Fucking Carmichael. He's never addressed me that way. I allow his tone and forgive him for being out of line due to his recent loss.

"I honestly don't know. But I will find out. You have my word, brother."

At least he's gone for now and can grieve in peace. Unlike me. I close my eyes, concentrating on ways to alleviate the pain while also keeping my anger at bay. I don't want to be here. I resent the fact that it is a necessary evil that in order to move our next shipment of guns, a huge party is needed. Plus, the Delta Pi Theta Halloween party is legendary, and everyone is expecting it—murders be damned.

This year, we locked down on who would be allowed to come, since parties are being shut down left and right, and also because that fucker Van Doren is back. And the other fucker, my fucking twin, Soren, is back. What is this? Fucking round two? A rematch of last year? Dammit to hell. Worse, the student body is living for the confidentiality of the party and the exclusiveness of it. If anything, the secrecy is making our party an even bigger hit than ever before.

A secret party, where everyone is chasing the high of getting caught, the location only revealed through a riddle that was sent via a mass text message. Security had already been tight after The Bloody Parade, but after the incident with the football player in the truck last week, the campus has officially and completely shut down. No classes. No games. No library, so I wonder what Taylor is up to...

I guess when you start losing a student every other week, it's bad publicity for the university. Either way, hundreds of students stayed in town, just for the chance they would receive a text for the Delta Pi Theta Halloween party.

I had to give it to Summer, she could nail the deets for a college party. I sent Lee to deal with her and incorporate the help of her sorority to arrange getting the text messages out. That was her only redeeming quality now that I think about it. Well, that, and she could suck the soul out of my dick. But we lacked any solid connection, which is why I ended things with her. I couldn't take her in my life any longer, especially since Taylor showed up.

"Are you seriously going to chase after her?!" Summer practically screams at me, and it takes everything in me to stay calm. I'm so tired of seeing Taylor run away from me because of Summer. I should have officially ended things weeks ago. I just didn't realize the girl was too dense to catch a clue.

"You just had your dick inside me and then you went out with her!" Her voice is shrill, and her eyes are glazed. I scan her face, taking in her shaking frame. My mind turns over her words.

"When?" I ask, keeping my voice calm. Her chest shudders.

"When what?"

"When did we fuck?" I bite out, and watch as my words make her flinch. Her arms cross over her chest.

"This is so childish, Steffan." Her blonde curls bounce as she shakes her head. "I can't believe you have the audacity to sit here and say that to me."

"I'm asking because I know for a fact that it's been weeks since I fucked you. I haven't touched you since I kissed Taylor." My words turn hard, and I enjoy the smugness leaving her body.

"Is that some sort of sick joke?" she screeches, tears filling her eyes. "You cheated on me! I knew it."

My lips curl at her insinuation. I'm a criminal, I've ended lives and not batted an eye. For The Illicit Brotherhood, I do those things. In all my life, I've never cheated at anything. I've never had to. A laugh escapes my lips. Summer's eyes gleam with rage when she realizes she can't get to me. Everything falls into place and finally makes sense. "You didn't fuck me, Summer."

"Oh, because there's someone else walking around with your face?" she throws back, her words heavy with sarcasm. I grin.

"Actually, yeah." I nod. "Soren just got back. I haven't had an opportunity to introduce you to him, but it appears you already know him. Intimately."

Her mouth snaps shut, and her eyes widen. "I didn't know! I would never do that to you, Steffan! I thought you said your brother left campus!"

I shrug, her words rolling right off me. If I truly cared at all about her, this would bother me. I feel nothing. "It's almost more insulting that you couldn't tell the difference between who you were fucking. We might share the same looks, but I guarantee you that our skills are different." I wink, and she blanches.

Her face pales. "I can make it up to you." Her hands go to unzip her dress, but I hold my hands up.

"I think we both knew this wasn't going to last, Summer. I've moved on. You should too."

"But it was a mistake, Steffan," she whines.

"It's over, Summer. See yourself out." I turn to my door and hold it open for her.

I haven't heard from her since, which is a fucking relief. It was over between us the second Taylor caught my attention. The minute I put my lips on hers, I became obsessed with knowing her, peeling back her layers to see who she truly is. Taylor challenges me, and not once has she sought to gain anything by knowing me. If Soren wanted to get back at me by sleeping with Summer, then that means he doesn't know about Taylor, and I intend to keep it that way.

I glance over the banister again, scanning the crowd below. Taylor isn't here yet. Somewhere, Soren is moving around, possibly as me, and that little bit of information puts me on edge.

"You should have a drink," Lee mutters from next to me, and my eyes slide his way.

"After last year? No fucking way." I shake my head.

Lee smirks. "There's no swamps nearby."

"Fuck you." I shove him, and he laughs.

"The pledges are all sober and monitoring. You have Suco making sure the kegs are exchanged, and we're in the middle of nowhere. No text messages went out to the football team." Lee goes over everything, but I'm still not relaxed. It's because of her. She could have decided that the Summer drama was too much for her. She could be lost, unable to find her way here. *She could be with Soren...* Does she know he's my twin? What if he is pulling the shit we used to do as kids, where we impersonate each other? If she does know, well, that opens all kinds of new questions. Maybe she's involved with my brother and part of all that's been going on. I laugh to myself and shake my head. Doubtful Soren knows Taylor other than as a girl I've shown interest in. I force myself to focus on the party, but really, I'm only watching for her.

The nice thing about Blue Rose is that there are many old, abandoned farm homes out in the country and on back roads. The pledges found one with a big-ass barn that was in decent shape, requiring very little cleanup, for tonight.

We've got a generator. Electric lights are strung all over the barn. Hay bales and lawn chairs for seating. Rows and rows of coolers filled with ice. A few troughs filled with ice and beers. Tables with finger foods. Music blaring. There aren't restrooms, but nobody seems to give a shit. Everyone is just happy there's a party.

The best and worst part is how secluded it is. No police. No complaining neighbors. However, if enemies wanted to hit us, we're easy targets and help is a long ways away. And right now, I'm not sure who it is we need protection from. Take your pick—Bryce, Soren, this killer on the loose who could be one of them, or some other enemy.

Having Taylor running around out here without me makes me feel jumpy. I'm not used to this feeling in my chest. It's more than just feeling protective, and for some reason, that only adds to the anger and fear I have at her not being here yet.

"Any sightings of him yet?" I turn back to Lee, keeping my voice hushed. He knows I'm referring to Soren.

Lee shakes his head. "Not yet. Although, he's apparently been able to fool half the brothers already."

Lee and I went back through the security footage and noticed that Soren has been back longer than I originally thought. He has repeatedly interacted with the brothers and infiltrated the Delta Pi Theta house, posing as me more times than I had anticipated. *Dammit.* My denial over my brother is causing me to underestimate him. I don't want to think he would do some of this shit, but here he is.

"Hey, there's Suco," Lee says, nodding his head toward the farthest end of the barn, where a hidden door leads to the kitchen.

I glance at Jose, who tilts his chin, signaling that the exchange went well. After the shitshow the past week has been, I feel my body relax just a fraction.

"See, I told you it would be fine." Lee steps back from the banister and readjusts his Devil mask. "Now, have a drink and try to enjoy some of the night." He smirks at me as he descends the wooden stairs. I watch through the haze from the fog machine as he makes his way over to some poor, unsuspecting girl dressed as an angel.

I'm about to follow Lee's advice, when a flash of red catches my eyes. I brace my arms on the banister, and that's when I see her. Despite the red lace mask adorning her face, I can feel it in my blood that it's Taylor. My gaze travels down to the red one-shoulder dress, draped skillfully over her body, all the way down to her Converse-covered feet. A grin pulls at my lips, taking her in, and something in me fucking snaps. I have to get to her. I want Taylor. Tonight.

I keep my eyes on Taylor as she and her friend move from the keg to the dance floor. I watch her body sway to the beat, her painted red lips permanently pulled into a smile, as she moves around the dance floor. My fingers itch to touch her, to feel the material of her dress shred between my fingers and finally have her against me. The crowd parts slowly with each step I take over to her, my lips twitching at how oblivious she is to being hunted. When our eyes do finally connect over her friend's head, she stops moving altogether, trapped with me in this moment. Her lips move, and her friend glances my way before moving away. My brow lifts, and Taylor takes the steps toward me, closing the space between us.

"I like the red." I bend close to her ear, making sure she can hear me. Seeing her skin pebble with goosebumps from the slight contact only heightens the tension between us.

"You seem to also like skulls." She tilts her head, eyeing me. "And blue."

Her choice of words throws me for a minute, my mind flipping from the half skull painted on my face, the blue tint to my hair, to the memories of last Halloween. The masks. The blue neon paint. The blood.

"Hades," I tell her. "Our school color is blue." I point to my hair.

Taylor's cheeks flush pink and she glances down before meeting my eyes again. I swear I see an apology flash in her eyes. "You're Hades?" I nod, my fingers coming up to my jaw as I study her.

"Persephone." She indicates with her hand, trailing over her own costume. I glance down, realizing it does resemble a toga.

"Guess Moira, the goddess of fate, is on my side tonight," I joke, and a small laugh escapes her.

"That was seriously corny." She shakes her head.

"Sorry. Couldn't help myself. Let me make it up to you by getting you a drink." *Smooth.* I am really working my charm here. She nods and then I place my hand on the small of her back.

I grab two bottles of beer as I lead Taylor through the barn and continue toward a less crowded area. There's a blanket thrown over some hay bales, and it's slightly darker in this area, which makes it the perfect location for us to get comfortable.

Taylor sits while I remain standing to open both our beers. I hand hers to her, but take a moment to admire her below me before sitting. She's beautiful and so damn sweet. There's a fire in her, and I love how she doesn't take any of my bullshit. This is the kind of girl I could give my tie to. But that kind of commitment is serious. That means I'd trust her with my secrets. Can I trust Taylor? What would Little Miss Good Girl think if she knew my hands were covered in blood? Those are the kinds of secrets that mean life or death.

"Are you okay?"

I blink and shake the thoughts away. "Sorry. Lost in my head."

I join her on the hay bale and she nudges me with her shoulder. "How'd you get lost in there? I figured it was all wide-open space."

"Oh! Taylor Mae with a burn."

"Do I need to go get some ice?"

"No, but you could give me a kiss to make it better."

Taylor groans. "Wow. I did not expect you to be so cheesy."

"I'm full of surprises."

"That, I don't doubt." Someone turns up the music. Taylor looks at me with an eager grin spreading from ear to ear. "Wanna surprise me with your dance moves?"

"By how bad they are?"

"By actually doing it." She stands up and gestures toward the swaying bodies. "Come on. Chicken?"

"Are you going to call me any other childish names if I don't?"

"I dare ya?"

"Dare?" Now that has my interest. "All right. I'll accept your dare."

I stand and follow her out to the open and dusty wooden barn floor that's filled with sweaty, dancing bodies. Taylor is the type of girl who isn't dancing to be sexy. She is genuinely wanting to be out here for the fun of it. But her body is still a little stiff. She's holding back. I ease closer to her and place my hands on her full hips.

"My turn," I whisper in her ear. There's a slight falter to her dancing, but to her credit, she doesn't give any other indication as to how nervous she is. I've been trained to notice every little tic and motion of a person. To pick up on any subtle hints. Otherwise, I might not have caught her falter. I smile to myself and continue, "I dare you..." I spin her around to face me. "I dare you to stop thinking. I want you to do whatever you want, right now, without a second thought."

"What are you talking about?"

"Don't give a single thought to anyone here. Not another thought about anything. Just do whatever you want." I stare down into her eyes. Challenging her to step more out of her comfort zone. Shed some of that prim-and-proper skin. Taylor licks her lips as she looks around. "Nobody gives a fuck, Taylor. They're too busy doing what they want. What do *you* want? Do it." She's still looking around, nervous. Like a little mouse. So

I repeat in a low, demanding voice, "Do it." Taylor throws her hands into the air and swings her hips. Then she bends her knees and drops down only to pop back up. Her eyes meet mine, and we both burst out laughing. "There you go!"

She dances with abandon, and I find myself eating up every laugh and smile she throws my way. Her hands are still in the air as I allow mine to glide down her sides and along her hips, and then back up. I bring her body firmly against mine. Taylor doesn't stiffen or pull away. Instead, she leans into me and allows our bodies to move together. My dick gets harder. I want her. I want her to be mine. But it's more than a physical attraction. It scares the hell out of me. Which is why I try to focus on those sexual desires, because if I think about this being someone I could see myself tied to—as in giving her my tie—it freaks me out. I have too much at stake. I have goals, demands, and a lot of fucking pressure. Yet, at the same time, I don't give a damn about any of that. Only her.

The song ends and Taylor pulls away with a huge smile. "I need a drink after that!"

We get her a drink, and I follow her back to our spot. "I guess neither one of us are the type to back down from a dare."

She pulls her phone out and then notices me watching her. "Just checking the time. But I couldn't help but notice there's no service out here."

"Nervous you won't be able to call for help?""Do you think I'll need to?"

I shrug and step closer into her space. "Want to get out of here?"

Her eyes widen, and her lips part. "Isn't this your party?"

I shake my head. "No. It's the people's party."

Taylor's eyes glance off to the side, and her hands fidget around her glass. "Don't you think after what's been happening, it might not be a good idea to go away from people? You know, safety in numbers. Potential witnesses. Help just a shout away."

I scan her face, noticing the worry in her eyes. "No. If anything, it makes me want to embrace the moment more and live. Cherish and spend it how *I* want to. How *you* want to. Do you really want to be back in that drunken mess?" She still looks nervous, so I say, "I won't let anything happen to you."

"That was one of the worst things I've ever seen. Finding Ava was hard. The Bloody Parade was one thing, but seeing him...he was trying to get away." Her breath hitches. I lean into her, my arms wrapping around her.

"I'm glad I didn't see the end," she whispers softly. "Thank you."

I freeze at her words, the pit in my stomach growing. Fucking Soren. "Come with me." Taylor leans back, her eyes still wary, and I can sense the rejection on her lips.

"You're not scared of me, are you?"

"No." Her answer is quick, and the blush is back in her cheeks. I smirk.

"Prove it." I step away and head for the wide, double barn doors. "I dare you!" I call out over my shoulder. The crowd of bodies separate to let me pass. After a few seconds, I can hear the tapping of her shoes on the wood floor behind me. Once we reach the outside, I take Taylor's hand and lead her to my motorcycle.

"Ah, Steffan..." She laughs and indicates the long skirt of her dress.

I stalk over to her and grab the material, ripping a slit up the leg, grinning while I help her on behind me. "Your place or mine?"

Taylor hesitates before answering, "Mine."

I take off, and her arms wrap around my waist. We speed out of the woods and back onto one of the old dirt roads. Gravel kicks up behind us, adding an extra denseness to the fog. If anyone is following us, I can't see them, but hopefully we're in the clear. I pick up speed and make a few unnecessary turns, taking the long way back into town, just to be safe. By the time we get closer to town, my adrenaline is spiked, and all I really want is to have Taylor all to myself. The weeks of sexual tension that have been building is like a live wire between us. Her little house off-campus comes into view quickly, and I hear the small hitch in her breath, because, of course, I know where she lives. Knowing everything about Taylor is becoming just as vital to me as breathing.

We get off the bike and stand with our chests pressed together in her driveway, the silence hanging between us while the air grows thick with lust and a hunger I've never known before. Our eyes lock while I trail my fingers up her arm, along her collarbone, and over her neck, before gripping her chin. Fear, need, excitement all pass through her expressive eyes, and her lips part slightly. Her tongue darts out to dampen the skin. The action calls to me, and I finally claim her mouth with my own. Her lips move against mine, my hand slides from her chin to cradle the back of her head, and my other hand grips her hip, bringing her body against mine. She moans and gives my tongue perfect access to slide in and writhe against hers. When her arms come up to circle my neck, the last of my control snaps. I grip her ass in my hands and haul her up my body, her legs wrapping around my waist while I carry her to her front door. Taylor shoves her key ring into my hand, and I manage to break away from her lips, long enough to suck air into my lungs and get the door open.

"That way, to the left." She motions with her hand before her mouth is back on mine, and she's biting my bottom lip before sucking it into her mouth to soothe the sting. My body hardens, and my need to be inside her grows even stronger.

I follow her directions, and soon, we're crashing into her room. I set her down on her feet, where she toes off her shoes and flings her mask to the side. I slide my jacket off, taking my time and watching her body tremble under my gaze. Her red lipstick is smeared over her mouth, and smudges of black and white from my own face paint peppers her skin. I reach out, and my thumb rubs the mixture of paint together, making a swirl of color over her jawline. Her eyes drag up my body, and when she meets my gaze, her pupils are dilated. My hands land on her shoulders, fingers digging into the material of her toga as I shred the remaining fabric. Right as I reach for her, her hands land on my chest, creating distance.

"Wait!" Her head falls forward. "Oh my God, we can't do this."

Everything in my body halts. "What's wrong?"

Taylor steps back, creating more distance between our bodies, and I can feel her starting to pull away emotionally. "Taylor. Look at me." Her eyes snap up, and I read the flash of shame that flickers there. "Talk to me."

One of her hands comes up to her mouth, touching her lips tentatively as if she can't believe mine were there only moments ago. "I can't believe we just did that."

"Why? I don't see what the problem is. You want me, and I sure as hell want you too."

"You have a girlfriend!" Her head whips up, her mortification evident.

I can't help it. I chuckle. "That's what you're worried about?" I finish unbuttoning my shirt and let the fabric fall to the floor.

"Steffan, this is serious. I don't condone cheating. I shouldn't have even kissed you before, but this—"

"Summer isn't my girlfriend," I tell her before she can finish her sentence. Hearing her say we can't and shouldn't be together is causing my anger to rise. "I haven't fucked her since we started hanging out."

Taylor's mouth drops open. "But she—"

"She said that to hurt you. I haven't touched her," I explain, leaving out the part that Summer thought she was having sex with me because my twin is running around campus unchecked. I grab the button on my pants and slide it through the hole. The fabric sags down. Taylor follows the motion with her eyes, and her teeth bite down on her bottom lip.

"Come here," I whisper.

She hesitates only for a second, before coming into my arms. Our bodies are flushed together as we both try to get as physically close to each other as possible. I lose my footing and take her with me as I fall onto the bed. Her sweet mouth giggles against my lips in surprise. I climb on top of her, my hands dive into her hair, my mouth attacking hers, stealing her air and running my tongue over hers. Taylor's hands grip my sides, and she presses her body against mine, almost painfully, as if she's trying to mold us together. Somehow, we both shed the last of our clothes and fall naked onto her bed. I refuse to let her go. My hands skim every part of her softness, while I trail my lips over her jaw and down her neck, biting where the flesh meets her shoulder. I want to taste her. All of her.

I roll onto my back and pull her body over mine. My hand snakes down between her legs, cupping her pussy and feeling her heat against my palm. I slide a finger against her slit and find her dripping. I groan and pump my finger into her. Her breath hitches, and she trembles, her hips bucking into my hand. "You're so tight and so wet." I pull my finger out and rub her juices against her bottom lip. "This is all for me, isn't it, baby?"

She nods her head frantically. "Yes."

"Good girl." I grip her hips and pull her body up, kissing along her stomach. "I want to taste you, Tay. I need to have my mouth on your sweet pussy while you ride my face."

Taylor moans, her body vibrating with need. I help her so her legs fall to the sides of my head, body hovering over my face. "Hold on, baby," I warn, before clamping my hands onto her sides and pulling her down. I use my tongue to lick along her folds, parting her and sucking her clit between my teeth. Taylor's legs shake and her head falls back, the long, dark hair brushing over my thighs. My cock hardens as I use only my tongue to spear inside her, eating her as if she is my last meal on earth.

"Oh God," she moans above me, her hands smacking the wall when she falls forward. I can feel her insides gripping me, her juices dripping down as she comes all over my face, chanting my name. I grab her hips and bring her down to the mattress.

"There's condoms in the drawer." Her voice is raw and thick. I raise my brow.

"Don't look at me like that," Taylor grins. "Kali stocked it on my behalf, she had hope for me. She's also stocked the bathroom. She's slightly crazy, but I love her."

I lean my body over to pull open the nightstand drawer. My hand dives into the drawer and I pull one out. Taylor grabs the foil packet from me and tears it open as she reaches for me. Her hand touching and stroking my cock is better than I could have imagined. Once I'm covered, I line up with her entrance and push inside in one go, filling her to the hilt. Her back arches off the bed and a gasp leaves her lips. My nerve endings are on fire, my chest coils tight with emotion when her eyes collide with mine. I cage her in with my arms, surrounding her head, and flex my hips, thrusting into her over and over again, reaching as deep as I can go. Taylor's hands grip my back, her nails piercing the skin, while her body moves with mine. Her pussy grips my cock tightly. I kiss her everywhere, her face, her neck, all over her tits, sucking one nipple into my mouth before moving to the other one.

"Steffan," she moans my name again, and I feel her getting wetter, pulling me in tighter.

I slide my hand between us and use my thumb to tease her clit. "Are you going to come for me, baby?"

She tosses her head back and bites her lip, answering me breathlessly, "Yes."

"That's my girl, come for me. I want your neighbors to hear you scream my name," I tell her against her mouth and watch while her orgasm finally rips through her, along with my name. Taylor's swollen lips part and her eyes darken when I thrust into her harder, our bodies sliding against the bed before I find my release too.

I swear I black out from the pleasure. We're both breathing hard when I roll off her. I want to stay and hold her, but I have to get rid of the condom first. I manage to find her bathroom and throw it into the trash. Damn, she's ravaged me. I feel thirsty and drink straight from the tap. The face paint from before is almost gone, so I quickly scrub the rest away before going back. Taylor is sitting up in bed, her face also fresh and clean, with a shirt on. I gesture toward the shirt with my unspoken question hanging in the air.

"I thought maybe you left," she says almost shyly, her fingers playing with the hem of the fabric. I can't help but stare at her, unsure of what to say. Normally, I would leave. I've never been into cuddling or sleeping next to someone. For some reason, though, leaving tonight, leaving her, feels like it would be the biggest mistake of my life. It's an odd feeling being so protective of someone who isn't family or part of The Illicit, and one I haven't been able to get rid of since she fell into my life. I can't leave her alone.

"Don't you think you have too many clothes on?" I shrug and give her a tilted smile. Her cheeks flush pink, but it only takes a few seconds before she tosses the shirt back onto the floor with our other pile of clothes. Such a good girl.

I swipe my phone up off the floor before sliding back into the bed with her. Taylor is hesitant, so I reach out and pull her down next to me. I set my alarm because, even though tomorrow is still the weekend, I have brotherhood shit to finish. Eventually, Taylor relaxes, and by the time I'm done texting Lee my location, she is fast asleep, her head pillowed on my chest. I can't breathe for a second while my heart beats too fast. I've never done this before. Tentatively, my arm wraps around her while the other curves under my head. It doesn't take long until I'm drifting off to sleep, listening to the sounds of nature outside and Taylor breathing beside me.

My last thought before darkness takes me, though... *Is that sound a hiss?*

CHAPTER THIRTEEN

Journal Entry – Oct 30th

I sit from afar, hidden in the shadows, watching with great amusement. Taylor is turning out to be quite the little minx. I bet she doesn't even realize she's sleeping with the snakes. Foolish girl. She's almost too easy.

Oh, I can't wait until all this unravels.

Soon...I could speed up the process, but where's the thrill in that?

I'm having too much fun right now. I think I'll play with Taylor a little longer. But soon, I'll have my revenge.

When they've all watched in horror at what I'm capable of.

When the fear is so deep within them that they become paranoid and sloppy.

When their grief is so strong from me slowly taking the lives of those closest to them.

When all of their fortune, which is rightfully mine, is back in my family's name.

When their very lives become mine to play with until I'm bored of them.

When they're bled dry...then I'll be able to rest.

Until then, I'll sharpen my blade and release the snakes.

Trick or treat, Taylor. Beware of those around you...you never know who's behind the mask.

CHAPTER FOURTEEN

Taylor

Clink. Clink. Clink. Screech. My eyes fly open. I raise my head and listen. *Clink. Clink. Clink. Screech.* The noise is coming from my window. A small part of me fears that *he*'s found me. Somehow, he knows where I am. And he knows I'm with the man who took what he considered to be his *precious gift*. Would his obsession really drive him here?

I slide out from under Steffan's arm. The old wooden floors creak under my feet as I stand. Grabbing my robe, I slide it on as I slowly walk toward the window. Through the thin white curtains, there's a shadow moving along the glass, but I can't make out what the silhouette is from.

I inhale a breath, hoping to gain the courage to pull the curtain back. Steffan is sleeping peacefully, but I know I should wake him. I'd feel silly waking him up, though, if it's only a tree branch tapping and rubbing against the window. I slowly count, trying to gain some courage. *One, two, three, four...* I drop my hand. I can't do it.

Clink. Clink. No. I'm being paranoid. Plus, Steffan is here. Kali has also probably made it home by now. I snatch the curtains and quickly jerk them open.

A scream is lodged in my throat as I'm caught between wanting to cry for help and wanting to vomit. There are three, long black snakes with red bellies sliding along my window. The source of the *clink, clink* noise is a glass box tapping against my window, hanging from a thin string that's connected to a branch next to the house. There's a tiny mouse running around, afraid. The snakes stretch across and press their noses to the air holes and continue to slither, circling their prey.

I can't. I can't leave the mouse there. Who would do this? Is this a trap...for me? To lure me out into the darkness. Is the mouse a representation of me? Only one person has ever referred to me as *Little Mouse,* and he's sleeping. This has to mean Steffan is not the killer. We could be the next victims, though. I cringe, remembering the last crime scene. I barely remember Steffan getting me to Kali's car after seeing the guy in his truck. It was weird because he wouldn't speak to me. Then again, he was probably just as shaken by the scene as I was.

"Steffan," I whisper. "*Steffan.*"

Suddenly the sound outside gets louder. I spin around to see the box is swaying even more. *No.* I shove Steffan, but he's sleeping hard. I don't have time to wait for him. Acting on stupidity and impulse, I run out of my room and continue out the back door. I halt in my tracks once the cold air hits me. What am I going to do now?

I hurry back inside and grab a broom, and then one of the kitchen knives. It's not much, but it's better than just me barefoot and in my robe. "Kali!" I yell as I begin to exit the house. "I need help outside! Steffan!"

The glass box has slowed its swinging, but the snakes are still trying to climb in it. "Leave him alone," I call out as if they'll understand me.

"What if this is how nature designed them?" I jump with a yelp at the low voice behind me.

"Steffan," I sigh in relief, "thank God you woke up."

He smiles...but it's different. I shake my head because he's probably thinking I'm nuts, so his smile is just forced. I honestly can't blame him. Then again, of course I am going crazy, because who ties a glass box with a mouse outside someone's window? A psycho, obviously.

I clear my throat as I take a cautious step toward the snakes. "This isn't how nature designed it, though. This mouse was trapped by someone and left to be slaughtered. And we're going to save it."

There's a tinge of humor in his voice. "We are?"

"Yes, *we* are."

"Last time there were snakes left for me, I called the police and they sent animal control. Turns out, these snakes aren't venomous, but I still don't want to get bitten by one."

"They're pantherophis obsoletus. Black rat snakes. So, of course, they'd be drawn to that sweet little mouse." I tilt my head, but I don't turn to look at him. There's a nagging in the back of my mind, a familiarity to the way he pronounced mouse. Chills break out on my skin as I feel him approaching me from behind.

He doesn't touch me, but he's close enough that I can feel his body heat. A sweet, woodsy smell with a hint of tobacco fills the air around me. *When did he smoke?*

Steffan takes the broom from me. "You don't need this. These snakes won't hurt you, Little Mouse."

I'm getting a strong sense of déjà vu; this is freaking me out. His blue eyes are hard, but there's a hint of mischief. They're not the deep, happy and light eyes he'd shown me earlier. These are the eyes that have filled my dreams since a year ago.

"Are there any snakes I should be afraid of?"

His response is a smile that promises danger and pleasure. He turns his back on me and walks directly to the glass box. The snakes coil back from him. One slithers away so fast that I lose it to the darkness as soon as I blink.

"Should I release him here?"

My jaw drops. "Of course not. Did you see how fast that thing is? He'll be dinner in no time."

Steffan's low, half-hearted chuckle stirs something inside me. "Then let's get to walking, so we can give him a running start."

"I need shoes." He looks down at my feet and frowns. "I have some flip-flops just inside the door."

I skip over to the door. I crack the door open and reach in to grab my shoes. When I turn around, Steffan has placed the mouse box on a chair and is eyeing one of the snakes.

Maybe it's us being alone out here in the darkness that's got me so anxious. Earlier was wonderful, and I always feel tingles around him. This—this reminds me of how he was the first night we met. Dark. Mysterious. A hint of danger. But a rough tenderness that I can't explain. He's always kind of scary, and people automatically take notice of his presence when he enters a room. But when he's like this, it's as if he can hide his presence until he's ready to strike. *Like a snake.*

He bends down and picks up the snake. I take a step back when he takes a step forward. "You're safe, Little Mouse."

"You haven't called me that in a while."

He doesn't answer, and I don't push the topic. Instead, I tentatively reach my hand out. The black snake with the red belly coils back, but I slowly ease my hand and touch my fingers to the top of its head. The scaly skin is smooth and cold.

"No more ganging up on tiny mice, buddy."

I step back with a start from Steffan's low laugh. I'd heard him laugh before, but this time it sounds different. When his eyes meet mine, he looks surprised by his own outburst. His eyebrows pinch together as his eyes turn angry. He bends down and releases the snake. Without a word, he grabs the box, and then I wordlessly follow him into the woods behind my house, using only our phones as flashlights.

The only sounds I hear are the pounding of my heart and the leaves crunching under our feet.

Steffan opens the glass box, and I watch as the little mouse hurries out and disappears under the brush.

"Should we make sure he makes it safely away?" I ask.

Steffan's icy eyes and perfect teeth shine bright in the darkness. "Shouldn't you be more concerned with your own safety? Who is going to make sure you get away?"

A person with an ounce of self-preservation—or common sense—would be alarmed by the change in his tone and the menacing words. Apparently, I'm not that type of person, judging by how my body is tightening and getting wet.

"Are you not confident in your abilities? Don't worry. I'll keep you safe," I quip with a smirk. I turn around, thinking I'm clever and going to leave him standing there with my smart remark. A hand comes around my throat, not hard, but enough to pull me back and lock me firmly against his chest.

"Oh, I'm *extremely* confident in my abilities. In all areas." His voice drops an octave and tickles the skin below my ear. "You should know."

I can feel his hard length pressing against me. A small voice is shouting at how wrong this is. *Red flag, you idiot! Run!* But that voice is so tiny, I barely hear it. My body sure as hell isn't listening. I'm practically purring under his hold. How could I even think for a second that he's Steffan? His name may be a mystery, but I know exactly who he is. He's the Masked V-Card Bandit. I'd been seeking him out, but here we are, a year later, only for him to be the one to find me.

"That's just it. I do know." I press my neck farther into his hand. Time to get him to admit to not being Steffan. "You've improved since last year. Much better performance *this* Halloween than our first time last year."

I'm poking the bear. No, I'm poking the snake. Unlike the ones from outside my house, this one *is* venomous. He will strike. Maybe that's why I'm trying to rile him... I want him to attack. Then I'll finally have the truth of who I gave my virginity to and discover if this is one big game to him and Steffan.

Those strong fingers tighten. His body is vibrating behind me. "Is that right?" He releases me with a light shove. I watch with disappointment as he begins to walk away from me. When I see his phone's light turn off, I try to follow after him.

"Hey! Don't leave me out here. Where'd you go?"

A voice calls from in the distance. "It's a straight shot to the house. Once you get out of the trees, it's not even that dark with all the lights from the street."

I try to go in the direction of the voice. "Aren't you going to go back to bed with me?"

"I'll meet you there."

"Why not walk with me? Did I bruise your ego that bad?" I can't hide my amusement. I mean, what did he think would happen when I got back to the house and mentioned what happened here tonight? Then I pause in my steps as a thought slams into me. More like a reminder that he could very well be the killer.

I'm out here in the middle of the night, and nobody knows it. I'm helpless... The thought sends a shiver of fear through me that keeps me frozen in place. A rustling from my left has me spinning in that direction, only to have him appear at my right.

"Are you scared, Little Mouse?" A strong hand reaches out and wraps around my wrist.

I gasp under his grip. "Why would a little mouse be scared while a snake circles her in the dark?" My breathing is so labored, and with him standing so close, my breasts rub against his chest with each inhale. "Is it because snakes devour mice?" I lean into him and whisper against his ear, "If you plan to make a meal of me, as you did last time, then I can only hope you decide to devour me again."

There's a low growl as he places his hand on my neck, and then he hisses, "Say it. Quit speaking in riddles and metaphors. You want me to fuck you. Right here. In the woods like animals. You could scream and nobody would hear." His hand on my neck travels up to my chin and squeezes. "But I would. I'd hear you scream out my name."

I shove his hand down and then speak against his lips. "Steffan...or your name?"

He stills. I love that I surprised him. The fact that he thought he had me cornered, deceived, and with the upper hand, but here we are. As it was a year ago, I'm here wishing I could see his face in the darkness. A face that looks *exactly* like Steffan's. Why didn't Steffan ever tell me he had a twin?

"You don't even know the name of the man you fucked? You gave your virginity so eagerly and willingly to a nameless face, so I shouldn't be surprised you jumped at the chance to spread your thighs for my brother." His voice has turned so cold.

I shove him away from me. "I thought he was you. That night. I saw you, or who I thought was you, walking with Summer. Then you disappeared. I searched for you everywhere." I wet my dry lips and then continue, my anger growing with each word, "Then you were in my class. Only it wasn't you. At first, I thought I'd imagined you wrong. It was your face...but different. The scent was off, but I ignored it. The kisses were both passionate, but the tastes, the heat, the tenderness..." I begin to feel breathless. "It was easy to fool myself that I'd found you, until you found me. Nobody told me there were *two* of you!" My breathing becomes rapid. "There's two. It all makes sense, but I have so many questions. Where have you been? Why hasn't anyone mentioned a twin?"

With each question comes another one. How many times has this twin impersonated the other one? I narrow my eyes. "You slept with Summer. When she barged in and was angry at seeing me there. Shine the light, so I can see your face." His face takes on an eerie and sinister appearance with the light under his chin. I watch as his eyes bore into mine as he slowly nods. "You were outside my house the night the snakes were in the bathtub." Another nod. "I fainted in *your* arms in the street." Another silent nod. "My house? This isn't your first time at my house."

"I was also at the library."

"Why?"

"Because I've been searching for you, too."

My entire body tightens. We've found each other, but now what? Steffan. Where does that leave us? I care for him, but I've not stopped thinking about...

I charge at him. "What's your name? Will you ever tell me your name?"

He chuckles and then turns off the flashlight. This time, he really does leave me alone in the woods.

CHAPTER FIFTEEN

Steffan

Something wakes me from a deep sleep. I don't know if it was the muffled shuffling of feet on the wood floor, or the sensation of being watched. With my eyes closed, I keep my breathing even and take in my surroundings. My fingers flex under the blanket, and I notice that Taylor isn't lying next to me. I don't smell her usual scent either, and I automatically know she isn't in the room with me at all. I mentally curse myself for falling asleep anywhere but at the frat house, and for making the decision to leave my gun in my room earlier. The floorboard groans, and I pop my eyes open.

"Oh shit!" Taylor's roommate jumps away from the door where she was standing. Her long reddish-brown hair is pulled into a braid over her shoulder, and I'm pretty sure I smell whiskey on her. When she wobbles, a goofy smile pulls at her lips.

"What are you doing?" I ask, sitting up, keeping the blankets around my waist. I cock my head to the side, staring, not fully trusting her yet.

"I should be asking you the same thing." She giggles, waving her hands around the room. "Didn't you leave here with Taylor a little bit ago? Did you leave her in the woods?" She snickers and stumbles back.

"What are you talking about?" I grab my pants off the floor, and she makes a big gesture of turning her back to give me privacy. I have zero fucks to give if she sees me naked, though. That's her problem for barging into Taylor's room.

"You and Taylor. You two went into the woods."

I don't ask any more questions. Chills skate over my skin while I grab my shirt and socks, before shoving my feet into my shoes and taking off out of the house. Yanking my phone out of my pocket, I try calling Taylor, but it goes right to voicemail. I try Lee, and the same thing happens. My eyes fall to my screen and I realize I have zero bars out here; the house is practically in the middle of nowhere.

There is a clearing in the backyard, and without thinking, I run into the open space, my eyes adjusting to the dark as I go. Crickets and toads sound off around me while I strain to listen for human noises. I follow the path farther into the woods, careful not to break any twigs or be too loud. My gut churns when I finally hear voices, knowing what I'm about to see. Everything slows, and a realization that I had been fighting against slams into me.

Taylor.

Soren.

She may be oblivious to my presence, but my twin is not. He gives me a small smirk, letting me know he sees me. Our identical eyes meet for a brief moment, and in his eyes, I see everything. The more I listen, months of memories flood my mind, finally making sense. Her look of surprise at seeing me in class, the accusatory slant of her mouth when she kept throwing out tidbits about Halloween and masks. The way her eyes flashed with hurt when she saw me and Summer in the stacks. It all fucking clicks. My brother had her first. Taylor thought I was him.

Anger floods through my veins and twists my insides, almost crippling me. Soren walks away from Taylor, and soon, she's heading in my direction. Her face is pale in the moonlight, and she shivers slightly in her robe. I force myself to cut off all feeling. By the time Taylor reaches me, I'm a void. Cold. Numb.

Her eyes flicker over my face, probably checking to make sure I'm me. She glances over her shoulder in the direction Soren disappeared. I scoff, and the noise brings her attention back to me. "Don't worry, Tay, you're with the right twin this time."

She sucks in a breath, and her cheeks flare pink. "Why didn't you tell me?"

I shrug. "Well, now you've fucked both of us, so it should be easier to compare notes."

She flinches, and I hate that I want to reach for her. The irrationality of my thoughts is not lost on me, but I can't help the feeling that's crawling around inside my chest. I just need to know. "Did you think I was my brother? Did you think I was Soren?"

She shakes her head, her eyes wide. "Yes. No. I don't know. I didn't even know his name." Both of her hands glide through her hair.

I nod and start to walk away. He must've fucked Summer to get back at me. The only difference is, I didn't know he'd already been with Taylor. She could've told me she thought we'd had sex. That we'd already met. Shit. *She* could've said anything. I thought she was different. This is why I don't do relationships. This is why I have never wanted to let anyone get too close and never felt anyone was worthy enough to let them in. I will live and die before giving away my tie. I've only heard of a few brothers handing over theirs in The Illicit, and now I know why.

"Wait! Steffan," she calls behind me, but I keep moving. She thought I was Soren. She's just another girl in the pond of sharks, who is willing to take any of us, not caring enough to know anything more. I make it back to the house, my eyes flashing to the front window where I can feel Taylor's roommate staring. I cock my head at her, and the girl shrinks back from the glass. I swear I see a ghost of a smile on her lips, but I'm not sure. Something in my gut twists, but I ignore it, fully set on getting as far from Taylor and her creepy roommate as I can. I jump on my bike and take off back to the house.

Back to safety.

"You've been a fucking ghost since you got back yesterday after the party," Lee confronts me. "Want to share with the class?"

I flip him off and continue walking down to the basement. While the drop had been largely successful, there was one person who thought he could outsmart us and cash in. These mafia brats never learn. Lee had already been in contact with our fathers, and fortunately, this time, we didn't need to spare the pledge. Their family had exceeded the number of times The Illicit were willing to overlook their indiscretions.

"Anything on Soren yet?" I turn to Lee, and he sighs, knowing I'm keeping something from him.

He shakes his head. "No one has seen him. Not that that means anything. Half of them didn't realize who he was the first time."

They aren't the only ones. I mentally shake myself, wanting to get out of these thoughts. Is my brother trying to hurt me on purpose? If he hadn't seen me, would he have tried more with Taylor in the woods? Would she have let him, thinking it was me? I don't know why it bothers me. I haven't heard from Taylor since yesterday. Since I left her in the woods, calling my name. I didn't reach out to her, and I don't know why I thought she would reach out to me. Stupidly, I had been thinking she was different, and that the weeks of banter and spending time together meant something. The image of her and my brother is forever burned in my brain. Anger flashes through my mind. My hand tightens on the door to the basement, and I yank the door open harder than I mean to. The voices from below hush, except for the whimpering of the low-level scumbag who thought he could steal from us and get away with it.

Everyone creates an opening as I walk through the crowd. As asked, Jeremiah is kneeling on the sheets of plastic that had been previously laid out. His body sways, and he pisses himself when he sees me. "I didn't do it! He's lying!" Jeremiah points to Suco, who meets my eyes above his head. My jaw tics.

"Blaming him isn't going to improve your case," I warn, my voice stern and detached. It's a message I hope everyone here takes into account. Suco's family may appear weaker with their lack of numbers and support, but they are still a force. I want Jose Suco on my side when our time comes.

Jeremiah's eyes harden, and I can finally see the deranged gleam in them. My gaze lingers on his skin...pale, blotchy, and full of scars and scabs. My guess is he thought stealing would help him get closer to the little addiction problem he has. The one his father warned me about. "Who helped you?"

Jeremiah shakes his head, a crazed smile spreading over his lips. "You have more enemies than friends on this campus, Carmichael. But if you spare me, I can help you with that."

I tilt my head, as if contemplating. Everything he already said, I know. It has always been this way, and it always will be. It comes with the territory. The only difference this time is that I don't know if my brother is friend or foe. My hand whips behind my back, fingers grasping my 9mm. I twist on the silencer, all the while ignoring Jeremiah's yelling of obscenities. I glance at him and move closer, placing the barrel between his eyes. "You give me a name and I might let you live."

He opens his mouth to speak right as I pull the trigger. Surprise flashes over his face for a brief second, as if he couldn't believe I didn't give him a chance. Jeremiah's body slumps backward, right into the mess of blood and brain matter behind him.

"Clean this up." I glance at the brothers and pledges around me. Half of them have respect registered on their faces, and a few look shocked. I whisper to Lee, "Take the remains down to the pond. Miss Allison will take care of him." Lee has become much more familiar with Allison over the past year. He's never mentioned his first encounter with her, though, and if he suspects Soren intended to kill Bryce that way, he hasn't said a word. Lee is one of the smartest guys I know. He continues to prove that and his loyalty, every day.

"His father didn't want the body back?" Lee questions with a small smirk on his lips.

I shake my head. "He'll be a nice snack for our friend."

I see a few of the pledges looking uncertain, but the brothers jump into action around us, rolling up the plastic and getting cleaning supplies. I look down at my arm and notice the red specks of back spray. I need a shower, and maybe some sleep. My phone vibrates and I take it out to check.

Dad: Did you remember to feed Allison?

Me: She's getting ready to eat as we speak.

Tucking the phone back into my pocket, Lee and I reach the top of the stairs.

"Ah, Steffan," one of the brothers meets me in the living room, "there's a chick here to see you."

I roll my eyes. "Tell Summer—"

"It's not Summer." The guy's eyes widen, and his hands come up.

"Where?"

"I had her wait in the study room," he explains, but I'm already taking off. I can sense Lee is following, but at a slower pace.

The door of the study is open, my eyes landing on Taylor pacing the room, her thumbnail stuck between her teeth. Her cheeks are pink, and when she looks at me, fire flares in her eyes, making her look more alive than the last time I saw her.

"What do you want, Taylor?" I ask, my tone bored, even though my stomach is twisting, ready to hang on her every word.

"You can't just leave and not let me tell you my side of things!" she accuses, her hands spread away from her sides. "I was the one who was left clueless. You both lied to me. I had no idea! Yes, I met Soren first, last year on Halloween. We slept together and he left. I had no idea what his name was or anything about you. I didn't hear from him or see you until this year. At first, yes, I thought you were him. I admit that. And maybe I was trying to convince my brain that I was imagining the differences, but I couldn't get that thought out of my head. The more time I spent with you, I felt it. Your hair is shorter. He smells like cigarettes, woods, and leather, and wears Converse. You smell like mint and expensive cologne, and I never see you in the same pair of shoes. Your eyes have a darker blue ring around the outside of the irises, where his is almost silver. You laughed with Lois, and I've never seen Soren have a real smile."

"Why are you here?" I stop her tirade before I do something really stupid, like pull her into me and bend her over the desk and sink balls deep inside her. She's making me crazy, and quickly changing the narrative of my thoughts from the last twenty-four hours.

Taylor huffs. "To tell you that despite whatever story you have made up in your mind, I did know the difference. But because you share nothing about yourself, I had no idea you were a twin, so all these inconsistencies didn't make sense. And I did like you, Steffan. Despite what you think, I don't go around just spreading my legs for everyone. I thought the other night meant something, but maybe you are just an asshole. And I'm the fuck-up who let you have a part of me."

She flings a packet of papers onto the desk. "Here's my part of the assignment. After Thanksgiving break, find a different partner."

Taylor rushes past me, out of the room, and I let her. My legs don't work and my mind spins. A warmth spreads in my chest, and I have no idea why.

"The fuck? Are you smiling?" Lee laughs as he steps into the room.

I glance up at him, shaking my head in disbelief.

"You're an idiot," he tells me, and I laugh. He points to where Taylor just left, and declares, "Seriously. I think I'm a little in love right now."

"Shut it," I tell him, picking up the packet she left.

"No. I'm thinking about going after her if you don't."

Ignoring him, I open the packet. It's our project that's past due, that we already have an extension for, and is due this week. I read where we left off, only to find STEFFAN IS AN IDIOT written over and over again for the next two pages. Lee falls into the desk laughing. She left me to do the rest of the assignment.

CHAPTER SIXTEEN

Taylor

Soren hasn't shown himself, but I sense him. I feel those cold blue eyes when I arrive and leave work. My house. And even yesterday, when I went to the frat house. The longer I think about it, the angrier I become.

How dare Steffan have the nerve to get mad at me because he found me in the woods with his twin, whom he told me nothing about? What, he's mad because I kissed him? Or because his brother had me first? Did he not tell him? How do I know this hasn't all been a game to them both? I mean, neither one said a word. They're brothers, after all, so I'm sure they've had a good laugh with all their frat brothers. My thoughts are everywhere, which is why I jump as I'm unlocking my front door, and look to find Soren leaning against the edge of my house.

"You're very jumpy."

"Sorry. I wasn't expecting anyone to be creeping around the side of my house. Have you been lurking in the woods again?"

A faint smile tugs at his lips. Those perfect lips. "No. You're always skittish. Why is that, Little Mouse?"

Maybe it's because I'm tired of everyone and everything, but I finally let it out. Let out the words that I've not said to anyone else before now. "I had a really bad relationship."

Soren stands straighter, and his eyes become more intense. *If that's even possible.* "Did he hurt you?"

Continuing on with my truths, I tell him, "No. But I was always afraid he would. He liked to hurt himself."

Soren stares at me and then does something unexpected. "Follow me." He turns and then disappears behind the house. I chase after him until we're out in the middle of the yard. "Drop your backpack and come and stand in front of me."

"Why?"

"You can't always be afraid. There's a murderer on the loose. You have some asshole ex. Bryce is still sniffing around you. Probably for information on what you've told the police. Especially because of what you know about us. Then the most dangerous predator...is standing in front of you." He gives me a half smile. "And unfortunately, there's two of us." *Of course there is.* He gives me a wink and then continues, "I'm going to teach you how to defend yourself, and hopefully kick someone's ass."

"Wh-what? Do you even hear yourself? I mean, this is crazy. You take my virginity, disappear for a year, pop back up with mice and snakes, followed by a weird encounter in the woods, and now a spontaneous fighting lesson in my backyard! Tell me you hear how crazy this all sounds."

He doesn't even blink. Soren simply places his feet apart and holds his fists in the air in a classic fighting stance. *Fine.* Let's do it. If anything, maybe this will prepare me for whatever crazy thing occurs in my life next.

After an hour of me getting my butt kicked, Soren allows me to take a water break. He follows me into the house, where I get us both a glass.

"Tell me his name."

I snort. "Why? What are you going to do? Kic—"

"Kill him," he interrupts me.

"That's not funny." Goosebumps spread all over my skin.

Soren takes a single stride, closing the distance between us. "I'm not the joking type."

"He never hurt me."

"Not physically, but he did enough damage."

"What do you care? We had one night together and that was it."

Soren places a hand on either side of the island behind me, caging me in. "Do you think I left you because I wanted to? I had every intention of making you mine that night. I *wanted* you. What I felt with you was different than anyone else. I don't let people in, Taylor. But I allowed myself just to be with you. We talked. We fucked. And I was making plans to do it again."

My heart is about to beat out of my chest. "Then what happened?"

"Steffan." He pushes himself away from me.

"I don't understand."

"Neither do I." Soren looks me up and down and then his lips press into a thin line. "I'll be back tomorrow."

Kali is helping me with a pizza when Soren walks into our kitchen like he owns the place. While holding a handful of shredded cheese, she's startled and yells at him, "Excuse me, motherfucker!"

"Soren!" I scold. "You could knock. How'd you even get in?"

"I told you I was coming back. Come on." He turns around and walks out of the room.

"Get a fucking bell on him," Kali grumbles as I follow after Soren.

As soon as my feet hit the pavement of the back porch, Soren spins around and grabs me. Instincts kick in and I elbow him as hard as I can in the ribs. I dig my heel into his foot and he growls, "Now kick the shin."

I do, and he releases me. His golden locks fall into his eyes, and he runs his fingers through them to pull them back. "Very well done."

We go over a few more techniques, and I hate to admit how much fun I'm having with him. And how excited my body gets with each touch. His words keep running through my mind, though. He didn't want to leave me. Soren wanted us to be more, he felt that night as much as I did. But what did he mean by Steffan happened? That night? Now? I still don't understand.

I pin Soren to the ground, but I don't get up. "What did you mean about Steffan?"

His lips go paper-thin again. His eyes are guarded. I press my forearm against his throat and apply pressure. Soren smirks. His face turns red and then almost purple. I release my hold for fear of him losing too much oxygen, and he laughs. He seriously laughs. He easily rolls me off of him and then pins me under his weight. "Steffan needed me that night. Brotherhood stuff. Then I...I was sent away for some family business."

"That sounds very shady."

"Maybe it was."

"Why didn't you come find me when you got back?"

"Why didn't you tell Steffan about what we did?"

"I thought he was you."

"But you never got angry at him that he didn't remember Halloween night?"

"I did! I hated him at first."

"Then what happened? Do you still hate him? Didn't look like it when he was fucking you. Or do you always fuck people you hate? I might have another go."

"Get the fuck off me." I shove at his chest, but he doesn't budge.

"You have to be ready for your opponent, even when you're angry. They're not going to only go after you when they know you're ready." I control my raging emotions and then use my strength and leverage to overpower Soren. And then for good measure, I kick the shit out of him and begin walking toward the house.

"Well done again." He chuckles. Then in no time, he's caught up to me. He takes me by the arm and spins me to face him. "I still want to know his name."

"Soren." I sigh.

"Please."

Something in the sound of his voice makes me pause. I feel emotions starting to swell inside me. "I haven't spoken his name in so long. I didn't want him to have that power over me. I thought if I buried his name..."

"The fact that you don't even want to speak it proves he still holds power. Don't give him any more of you than he's already taken."

"Alex. His name is Alex. But he's back in Mississippi, and I know I'm safe here because he was adamant about this not being the university he wanted to attend. He didn't want me coming here either."

"I'm glad you didn't listen to him."

"Me too."

Soren begins walking backward, away from me. "Maybe tomorrow I'll get his last name."

"Maybe." I watch him turn around and walk until he disappears behind the house, my heart beating in anticipation of seeing him tomorrow.

But the next day, Soren doesn't show up.

Or the next.

CHAPTER SEVENTEEN

Steffan

The satisfying splash of body parts hitting the water should make me feel calmer—another problem has been averted—but tonight, it's not working. I watch the water for the telltale sign that the beast who lives there is moving her way toward the snack I just left her. What a shit day. I'm down another pledge, and I haven't talked to Taylor in a while.

Taylor. She's at the forefront of my mind these days, but I'm at a loss of what to say to her. Part of me understands where she is coming from, while the other part still wants to blame her for not being exclusively mine. I'm so lost in my thoughts and turmoil that I don't sense him right away...until he's already behind me.

"Is it me, or is Allison looking a little overfed these days?"

My head falls back and a sigh leaves my lips. "What the fuck are you doing here?"

"Is that any way to treat your brother, really?" Soren scoffs, his tone laced in sarcasm.

"When my brother shows up, and not this dickhead, I'll make sure I hug him," I reply.

Soren's lips twitch. "But seriously, why does Allison look like she's eaten so much lately?"

"Because, you fuckstick, we've had a lot to clean up. The pledges this year aren't exactly doing themselves any favors. If anything, I feel like this is an execution year." I run my hand through my hair. "What are you doing here?"

Soren's eyes narrow. "Why? Sad I disrupted the little lovefest you had going with Taylor? Or Summer? I forget which girl you like getting your dick wet with more."

I take a step toward my twin and his eyes light up with the challenge. "Leave Taylor out of this. If you're pissed at me, just say it. I won't apologize for making you leave. If I hadn't, The Illicit could have come after you. Bryce almost didn't survive."

"Like I care about that knuckle-dragging asshole. He had it coming. His whole family was conspiring against The Illicit. All our father had to do was show the evidence, and they wouldn't have cared if I fed him to Allison. But no, dear ol' Dad turned to you, and your first thought was to exile me." Soren's eyes blaze with every word he speaks.

"Yes, they would've cared if you fed him to a fucking alligator! And I didn't exile you! It was a fucking break away, while we figured shit out here and things calmed down. I didn't want to do it either, I was told to make the choice, and it seemed what was best for you," I tell him, trying to knock some sense into his head, but my brother is stubborn.

"What was best for me? How was that best? Sending me away from everything I've ever known?" He grips his hair and then pulls before he extends his hands, pleading for me to understand.

I shake my head, completely at a loss for words. I knew this day would come, and I knew I would have to answer to him. I just thought he would be more reasonable about it. "I was worried. I knew you pushed Bryce toward Allison on purpose. If he had died, you would have been brought before the elder members of The Illicit. If someone had the slightest beef with our family, they would've used it as an opportunity. Something worse than sending you away for a year would have happened, and you know it. They might have fucking *killed* you. We don't get to make the rules, we just live by them."

His head tilts back while he breathes in and then exhales. When our eyes meet again, I see the anger has died down some, but so has a tiny bit of the respect I used to see there. Soren reaches for his pack of cigarettes and lights one before taking a hit. "Fuck, fine. Well, I'm back now."

I shrug. "Ummm... Okay."

We both watch the water as Allison finishes devouring her treats, the slap of her tail indicating she's happy with what I brought her. The more I think over the pledges, the murders, and the timing, it kills me to ask, but I have to know. "Is it you?"

Soren grunts. "Every drop of blood I've ever had spilt has been clean and to the point. Always for a reason. You think I really would take the time to display a kill? That football player was literally strung up by his insides. The homecoming queen, the guy in the truck, fuck, even the dorm girl was swimming in a bed of her own blood."

"Ava," I say her name out loud.

"What?"

"The girl who was killed in the dorms. Her name was Ava. She was Taylor's roommate and friend," I tell him. Our eyes clash again and I see his nostrils flare slightly when I say her name. Our shared obsession.

"Is that how you met?"

"No. We were partnered up for a psych class." I laugh, thinking back on it now. "She hated me right away, and I couldn't understand why. Makes sense now."

He shakes his head, his blond hair swaying slightly. "Something changed in me that night. All I could think about since I've been away was her. I wanted to find her after the party, but, well..."

"I get it," I tell him. I've been feeling the same way since Taylor literally fell into my life.

"I'm not going to give up." He throws it out there and my chest constricts. "Guess it will be up to our little mouse to decide."

I raise my brow. "Taylor isn't a game. She isn't a prize to be won. I will respect her decision."

If she chooses my brother, I will accept her decision, but that doesn't mean I'm not going to put up one hell of a fight to make her mine either. She showed me her strength when she put me in my place. A flash of Taylor wearing my silk blue tie around her neck dances in the back of my mind. For once, the thought doesn't make me want to run in the opposite direction. It feels right, like it's meant to be.

Another twig snaps near us. My hand reaches in my back pocket, my fingers running against the steel butt of my gun.

Dad.

"I figured you'd both be here." Rhett Carmichael steps out of the shadows. His business suit is slightly worn, indicating he must have come right from a meeting with The Illicit to be here. I glance from our dad to Soren and notice the hostile glare my brother is giving him.

"It's a little family reunion," I reply, my words heavy with sarcasm.

Dad looks from Soren to me. "When the campus shuts down because of some serial killer, you can't expect that our associates are going to just relax because you say you have it handled."

"Did you come here thinking I was the one doing it, too?" Soren asks, his voice hostile.

Dad glances at him, then me. "I taught you better than that."

Soren scoffs and I fight to hide my smirk. "I already told you I'm handling it. Maybe your associates should focus more on their own family lines."

He rolls his shoulders, the suit jacket flexing as he does. "Dupree's long-lost grandson has been found. He's sending him here to help clean up and get the campus running again."

"What the hell?" Soren breathes out. "A Dupree?"

Our dad shrugs. "Apparently, his mother took off with him when he was a baby. Tried to raise him righteous and on the straight and narrow, but he did some digging and found his way back to the fold. He's a year or two older than you both and has been studying law, so maybe he will be able to help some."

"This is insane." I run my hands through my hair, the pressure starting to cave in around me again.

"Well, you have a few days until he will be here. If I were you, I'd get things in order so the Duprees have no reason to think they can step all over us." Dad glances at the water, but his meaning is clear. "Is Allison pregnant or something?"

"Fuck you both," I grit through my teeth. Soren snorts, choking on his laughter. I glare at both of them, because fuck them. I've been here and dealing with all of this... The Illicit's associates' heirs, who don't know their dicks from their Glocks, who end up as alligator food. So, yeah, Allison looks fucking pregnant.

Dad chuckles and claps me on the shoulder, then turns to walk back into the woods, the way he came, before turning around. "Oh, I almost forgot. Maybe give Allison a break for a few days. Let her save some room. The vote was unanimous... the Van Doren kid...well, he needs to disappear once and for all."

Fucking finally.

CHAPTER EIGHTEEN

Taylor

I'm furious that I let myself fall for both of them, and then they both ditch me. I don't see or hear from them for weeks. Slowly, our campus decides to open up again. Because why not? There's been four murders, no one has been caught, but money still needs to be made, I guess. I'm working in the library when I hear a throat clear. "Well, if it isn't Thing One," I snarl. Kali was right. Soren really needs a bell around his neck. He gives me a half smirk, and heaven help me, if it isn't the sexiest thing I've ever seen. I wait for him to speak, but he doesn't, simply keeps staring. "Can I help you?"

He casually walks toward me. A very lazy, yet confident, walk. He's wearing dark denim jeans, a white button-up that's only buttoned halfway up, and his black Converse. His hair is messy, and his features seem sharper with his permanent scowl. While Steffan could pass for a fallen angel, Soren is nothing short of a demon coming to claim my soul. They may share the same face, both emitting a certain dominance and power, but where one wants to own my body, the other wants to consume my soul.

And with each step, I feel my defense lowering. *Or maybe that's just my knees.* I repeat myself, forcing my voice to remain firm, "Can I help you?"

"I think you might be able to."

He wraps his hand around my neck and presses my back into the history section. His lips punish mine in a hard kiss. When I don't open my mouth to grant his tongue access, he nips my bottom lip. He then uses my gasp to slide his tongue against mine. My traitorous body relaxes, and I begin to feel a wetness between my legs, but I force myself to come to my senses.

Shoving him hard, I only manage to unlock his lips from mine, which causes him to take a single step back. "How does that help you?"

"I've had a shitty day. And sliding inside of you," he takes a lock of my hair between his fingers, "might make it better."

Might? Gee, thanks, asshole. I narrow my eyes, and in a dry tone tell him, "I'm sure it would."

"I said *might*. Only one way to find out."

"I'm certain it would be the highlight of your day, week even. Unfortunately, you won't be finding out." I shove my shoulder into him as I walk past to finish my job. "You'll spend all night—"

Soren grabs me by the crook of my elbow and pulls me back to him. His hand grabs my hair painfully as he forces me to stare into those blue eyes. "Tsk. Tsk. Little Mouse. You think you can scurry off?"

"Soren." Steffan's voice is deathly quiet. "Let her go."

"Or what, *brother?* Will you call Father? Have you already alerted your little minions?"

Clearly these two only know how to growl at each other. There's definitely some family drama going on here, and I want no part of it. I jerk my arm free. "I don't know what family crisis is happening here, but I have a job to do. If you'll walk back that way, take a right, and go past the coffee station seating area, that second aisle is our self-help section. There's a couple of books on family counseling that might do you both a world of good."

I begin walking again, but this time, Steffan stops me by stepping in front of me, effectively blocking my path to freedom from this bizarre situation.

"We need to talk." His voice is low. "I'm sorry. I had no right to behave the way I did. Summer hadn't been able to tell the difference either, and I'd assumed—"

"You assumed I was like her. Really? I'm even more insulted. Thanks." Another smart mouth response is on the tip of my tongue until I feel a warm presence behind my back. I remain completely still as Soren moves closer, and closer, until he is fully pressed against my backside. I clear my throat as I place my hands on Steffan's chest to try and make room for myself. "O-kay. As I've mentioned several times, I have work to do...so if you'll excuse me."

There's an energy crackling around us. The quiet library. Their warm bodies pressed firmly against mine. I feel the rise and fall of their strong chests against my front and my back. I raise my eyes up to see them both staring down at me. The heat burning behind their eyes making my body quiver.

Steffan's hands cup my face. "I don't want you to be angry with me. Don't push me away."

Soren's hands grip my hips and press my backside against his raging erection. His lips dip to my right ear, the warmth of his breath tickling me. "You can be mad at me, Little Mouse. In fact, give me all your fury. I *love* when things get heated. Let me help you release all that pent-up energy."

"W-weren't you both mad that I'd slept with each of you? Unknowingly at first, and a year apart, I might remind you."

Steffan's forehead falls to mine. "That was our fault. And you don't know how much it means to both of us that you can tell us apart."

"And you don't give a shit about our last name," Soren grumbles.

"Let us apologize for how we acted. We live a life built around secrets. It's hard for us to do anything more than the bare minimum of communication."

Apologize? Didn't they already do that? My heart is beating against my chest as I see that they're wanting to express their sincerity with more than words. Soren's hand slides from my hip to the front of my flowy maxi dress. He reaches lower and gathers the material in his fist and begins pulling it up. Steffan lowers to his knees and ducks his head under the material Soren has in his hand.

With his other hand, Soren takes my chin and jerks my head back to look at him. His mouth is hot with desire. As his tongue massages mine, I gasp into his mouth when I feel Steffan's hungry lips tasting my arousal. This is wrong. So very, very wrong. My body isn't agreeing with my mind because it's begging for more. I want them both. God help me. I want them *both*.

A voice from my past interrupts the moment. He barges through my blissful haze, and my entire body locks up. Soren pulls back first.

"Steffan, stop."

Shameful tears fill my eyes. I try to turn my face, so they don't see them, but Steffan takes my chin into his hand. "What's wrong? Tell me. Did we push too far?" I shake my head and try to force myself from his hold. "Stop it and talk to me."

I squeeze my lips tighter together, and feel the pressure of years of ridicule weighing heavy on me. What have I become? What have I allowed myself to turn into? Why did I like it so much? I crave their touch. I desire their heated kisses, their hard bodies, and their throbbing cocks.

Even though I know it's wrong. It's more than that. So much more. *It's illicit.*

Soren shoves me into Steffan, then steps around, so he can face me. "Is it me? Do you only want my brother now?"

The look on his face is breaking my heart. "No. No, no, no." I force the words out. "I want you both. I've become my parents' worst nightmare. He's going to punish me...if he does to me what he does to himself..."

A dangerous energy crackles around us. Soren's voice has the hairs on the back of my neck standing. "Who? Alex?"

"Who. Is. He?" Steffan's voice lowers and takes a hard edge. "Nobody will hurt you. Now answer the fucking question."

"He is...was...my ex-boyfriend. I was supposed to remain pure."

They both give me a smile, that's as equally terrifying as it is exciting. Soren whispers as his fingers dance along my neck, "Tell me, Little Mouse, do you like us playing with you?"

Steffan takes a step into my space. "This *boyfriend*... Is he someone you still want?"

I shake my head. "I don't. I hate him. I—I want..."

"She craves the illicit. Don't you, Little Mouse?" Soren practically sings.

I nod, causing Steffan's smile to grow. "Then, let's give it to her, brother."

My body hums as I stand in the center of Steffan's room. Soren and Steffan circle me. I'm waiting with anticipation for one of them to strike. I'm not at all prepared when they both come at me at the same time. Steffan grabs my face and claims my lips, while Soren presses his front against my back to suck on my neck.

I can't even focus on one or the other. Warm, strong hands remove my clothing. Their lips seem to be everywhere at once.

My body is lifted and carried to the bed. I feel as though I'm being worshipped. Especially when I feel the heat of a tongue between my legs. I know this has to be wrong. It *is* wrong. A small part of me worries for my soul because I'm ninety percent certain it is leaving my body in this moment. My toes curl and I go straight as a rod with my knees locking when I feel my clit being sucked on. Another tongue is busy lapping at my nipples. A set of strong hands hold my hips down in place as they buck against a face. The other set of hands massage my breasts while kissing every inch of my skin. Oh my gosh, I don't even know who is doing *what*.

I begin to mumble a prayer. The one who's between my legs stops; the other one does as well.

"Please forgive me. Amen."

I open my eyes and look down at my nude body, and then at Steffan and Soren. It's Soren who is—or was—tongue-fucking me. Good to know.

"Were you seriously just praying?" Steffan asks.

"Thanking God for the blessing I'm about to bestow on your pussy?"

I place my hands over my face. "I'm going to hell in a hand basket."

"Sweetheart, you of all people are not going to hell," Steffan declares.

"Look at us! Steffan, look at me. This isn't how I was brought up. I'm having sex with two guys...twins...at the same time!"

Soren flicks me with his tongue and then says, "That sounds to me like you're God's favorite. Not everybody receives such a gift."

"You must've done something good. Really good. Let us carry out your blessing." Steffan grins.

"This is the Devil's work," I moan as they both continue doing wicked things with their tongues.

"She's called out God and Satan. Think we can get our names next?" Soren asks.

"Wanna make a bet to see which name she calls out first?"

"No! Stop! Staaaa—" I cry out as Soren inserts two fingers inside me. He continues to suck and lick me mercilessly, his fingers moving in and out of me. He then slides them out and spits on them. He goes back to alternating between running his tongue along my clit, and then sucking on it with his mouth, while his now lubricated fingers work my forbidden hole. I twist beneath his hold. The sensations overwhelming. It's building and building, until finally, I cry out, "Soren!"

I hear Steffan, who has been giving tender affection to my breasts, mumble, "Fucker."

When I come down from my high, I register Steffan telling Soren, "It doesn't count. You had access to more of her than I did."

Soren finishes licking up the remains of my orgasm, then responds, "I could've had her coming with her breasts, too."

"If you're both finished..." I grumble. "While I appreciate the orgasm, it's not a contest." Although, I think no matter who wins, I'm the sole victor in this one. Regardless, it's still awkward.

"Sorry," Steffan says. Soren only smirks.

"Can we take a break? I need a minute." I slide off the bed, and hurry to the bathroom. What am I doing? I've only ever had one boyfriend, and now I may have two at once? This is too much. They're brothers, at that. How will this even work? My mind is racing. I need fresh air. I grab a robe that's hanging in the bathroom and sneak outside.

I look up into the now night sky. It's so beautiful. The stars are shining bright since their fraternity house is in the middle of nowhere, surrounded by trees and water.

"You look so beautiful."

I gasp as my blood turns to ice. I know that voice. I've heard it sing many times in church, its holier-than-thou timbre in direct contrast to his actions. I spin around and stare in horror.

"Alex."

He walks toward me, his large frame towering over me. He's still so handsome. Dark curly hair and gray eyes that shine brightly against his light brown skin. My eyes widen. There is no way he can really be here. I glance back at the house, my lips open to scream, when I see them. They must have been watching me. I feel my legs tense, ready to give out.

Soren and Steffan step right in between us. Steffan's arm wraps around my waist and pulls me behind him. Their eyes are on high alert as they take in Alex, who smirks and makes a move to advance on us. Clearly, he must have a death wish.

"Get the fuck away from her." Soren pulls a switchblade out of his back pocket.

Steffan levels Alex with deadly eyes. "You have no clue who you're fucking with right now."

Alex chuckles. "I don't think you two do."

Soren scoffs. "I'm guessing you're Alex, the ex-douchebag."

Alex's gaze runs over my face when I peer at him from behind Steffan. "Tell them what my last gift to you was."

I swallow and frown. "Why?"

"Tell them, Precious. It's okay," Alex coos, and I shudder.

"It was a bear. A teddy bear."

"Go on..." Alex encourages.

"It had your favorite blue tie." I'm so confused as to why all this matters.

"Did you put the tie on?" Alex is now smiling at the twins as he asks me. I nod, and then I watch as their faces go pale. "Allow me to formally introduce myself. My full name is Walter Alexander *Dupree*."

What? His first name is Walter? "No. I've known you for years. You—you—how could I not know your first name is Walter?"

"My family keeps our full names hidden. For our protection. My great-grandfather went to great lengths to ensure our safety. Then my mother wanted me to have a clean life and eternal salvation. That's why I wasn't allowed to attend this school."

Steffan steps aside, and my heart breaks. He is moving out of *his* way. Leaving me defenseless. "But if this is what you want, Taylor, then I'll do it. I'll take my place."

"Your place?"

Alex—or Walter—runs his knuckles along his jawline, his eyes turning glacial. "Shush, shush, shush. Don't worry about them. They can't do anything. You don't know what the name Walter Dupree means, do you, Precious?"

"Lois's true love?" I answer, feeling like an idiot. I'm in shock. I haven't even had a chance to process *him* being here, and now he's connected to Lois? Why aren't Steffan and Soren looking like they're staring at a ghost?

"I'm *your* true love. And as such, I'll take my place as the head of The Illicit Brotherhood." He studies my face and chuckles at my confusion. "Did they tell you who they really are? Sinners. Murderers. A secret society of organized crime and greed. My great-grandfather founded it, making me from the original bloodline. Means little to you, but it's a big deal to them that I'm the descendant of Walter Dupree. Puts me at the top of the hierarchy. And you wear *my* tie."

He says it as though I should be honored, *proud* even. *None of this makes sense.* I'm so frustrated, scared, and confused. What does the tie have to do with any of this? The head of a fraternity—some secret society of murderers? He's lying. No. Steffan and Soren aren't denying a word of it. In fact, the twins look like they're going to be sick. Does Lois know about him and what became of Walter? Is Lois's true love Alex's great-grandfather? I have so many questions running through my head.

"I don't understand." I keep whispering, glancing from Steffan and Soren, who look like their world is crashing down, and then back to Alex. "I don't understand. *I don't understand!*"

"It means," his eyes flash, his lips twisting in a sinister smile, "I own you." I slap his hand away and rush to Soren.

Alex's voice turns cocky as he tells me, "They're not going to do a damn thing about it." He turns to smile at the twins. "Because I own them, too."

Soren shakes his head. "Fuck that."

Steffan grabs Soren's fist that was ready to strike Alex. "You can't."

Alex charges toward me. He grabs my arm, but I'm not the girl he knew in Mississippi. I twist in his hold and rear my head back into his face as hard as I can. Then I put as much weight as possible into elbowing him in the stomach. I stomp on his foot, and then spin around to knee him in the groin.

"Nobody owns me," I hiss. Then I take his face into my hands and shove my knee into his nose.

I don't bother looking at Steffan or Soren. Instead, I run. I run as hard as I can away from them, from Alex, and the messed-up brotherhood that I know nothing about. My bare feet squish under the muddy soil, but I don't stop. I run through the woods, over roots and obstacles that I won't allow to stand in my way. I have to escape. Alex has come for me. Has he been the killer all along? Worse, I don't know if Steffan and Soren will now take *his* side. Steffan sent his own brother—his *twin*—away for this fraternity. Will either of them choose me...or will their loyalty remain with their brotherhood?

It's all too much...so I do the only thing I know to do and that's to keep running. Something in me snaps as I struggle to get oxygen into my lungs. I'm running now to get away. But I won't run forever. I've already done that once. If they—no, *when* they come after me, I will fight back. I'll destroy *him,* them, and anyone else who thinks they can own me with some fucking tie.

In fact, I'll hang them with it.

Smoke the Enemy coming soon...

OTHER BOOKS BY GAIL HARIS

Stand Alone Novels

Arrogant Arrival (A Cocky Hero Club Novel)
Ashes (An Everyday Heroes Novel)
Allegiance (A Salvation Society Novel)

THE RANDALL SERIES

Who is Sarah Randall?
The Night That Changed Rachel
The Blackmail of Denise

K.O. Romance Series

Worth a Shot
My Best Shot
A Clear Shot

CO-WRITTEN GAIL HARIS & ASHTON BROOKS

THE ILLICIT BROTHERHOOD

Pledge Your Loyalty

Subscribe for Gail Mail! Don't miss out on release announcements, exclusive giveaways, behind-the-scenes snippets, and glimpses into the chaos of her life, and more!

GAIL'S NEWSLETTER (SENT ONCE - TWICE A MONTH):
Join now by clicking here (https://bit.ly/HARISNL).

OTHER BOOKS BY ASHTON BROOKS

The Midwest Boys Series
#MNGirl
My #MNGirl
#SummerGirl
#NYGirl Rogue- The Beginning

The Hearts Series Duet
Hearts and Bruises
Hearts and Flowers

Scar

Where Demons Hide

Warrior - A Salvation Society Novel

ABOUT GAIL HARIS

GAIL HARIS believes in fairytales, love, and laughter as the best medicine. However, she enjoys writing murders, laughter, and steamy happily ever afters.

She loves living in her small town in Southeast Missouri, and then taking adventures all over the world with her two wild and fierce princesses and Boo Bear aka her ultimate real-life book boyfriend and high school sweetheart, Bobby.

When she's not getting into mischief or scheming with her two girls, she's busy coming up with crazy scenarios for her characters. Using coffee and her imagination, Gail writes contemporary romances that blend laughter and true love out of everyday chaos while incorporating her warped sense of humor and awkward charm. She writes in a variety of genres, including romantic comedy, romantic suspense, and new adult/coming of age romance.

Hopefully, by following her own dream of becoming an author, she can be an example to her daughters that dreams can become a reality.

Never stop believing in love, dreams, and yourself. And coffee...don't forget the coffee and books.

Connect with Gail
WEBSITE : gailharis.com
FACEBOOK https://www.facebook.com/authorgailharis
FACEBOOK GROUP GAIL'S BOOK BELLES
https://www.facebook.com/groups/gailsbookbelles
INSTAGRAM https://www.instagram.com/authorgailharis/
BOOKBUB https://www.bookbub.com/authors/gail-haris
GOODREADS https://bit.ly/GRGAILHARIS

AMAZON AUTHOR PAGE https://bit.ly/GAILHARIS
TIKTOK https://www.tiktok.com/@gailharis

Subscribe to GAIL'S NEWSLETTER (TWICE A MONTH):
https://gailharis.com/newsletter/

Want to help promote Gail and possibly receive ARCs?
Join GAIL'S MASTER LIST!: https://bit.ly/GailMasterList

ABOUT ASHTON BROOKS

AM BROOKS is an author with a variety of stories; Contemporary Romance, New Adult, and mature YA Her writing style is suspenseful and sometimes leads to heart-wrenching conclusions. With a background in forensic psychology she really goes for those investigative, dark and twisty feels. And of course, lots of love!

Brooks enjoys reading as much as writing. Television shows such as *Criminal Minds, Scandal*, and *One Tree Hill* are her go-to binge worthy series. She loves spending time with her friends and family with a good glass of beer or wine. If she isn't reading or writing, Brooks is Pinteresting future home projects for her wonderful husband to accomplish.

Follow Me!
Website: https://www.ambrooksbooks.com
Newsletter: https://mailchi.mp/ea5fc7a2a98c/
ambrooksnewsletter
Facebook: https://www.facebook.com/ambrooksbooks/
Twitter: https://twitter.com/brooksauthor |
@brooksauthor IG: https://www.instagram.com/
ambrooksbooks/ | @ambrooksbooks Goodreads:
https://www.goodreads.com/user/show/93577252-a-m-brooks

Join my reader group to get all your info first!
Ashton's Rogue Readers: https://www.facebook.com/
groups/625793331210669/

Made in the USA
Monee, IL
23 June 2022

98463723R00122